Silent Sam
And Other Stories

Alan Arkema

MUSCATINE, IOWA

Published in the United States by Pearl City Press
An imprint of Writers on the Avenue

This is a work of fiction. All characters, incidents, and events are products of the author's imagination or are used fictitiously with no relation to actual persons or events.

For permission to reproduce selections from this book, contact Pearl City Press pearlcitypress@writersontheavenue.org

10 9 8 7 6 5 4 3 2 1

ISBN: 978-1-7369498-9-4

CONTENTS

SILENT SAM

Sketch found in Sam's Saddlebag

1 SAM

NOBODY KNOWED his name, his real name, that is. Least ways, we din't think we did. Why I say that'll come out as I tell his story the way I knows it. Even that ain't much. But I think I got to tell it. I ain't goin' to give out many names of folks and places when I tell it. Sam wouldn't like that. I'm sure he wouldn't like my tellin' you as much as I will be.

Still, I think it needs to be told for the sake of justice for Sam. That'll come out in my story too. Least ways he ain't goin' t'get no justice in this old world no other way and that's why I got t'tell it. I don't know why it's me doin' it 'cept if I don't nobody else will neither, and it needs to be told to set the record straight for Silent Sam. That really is the onlyest justice he'll be gettin', 'pears t'me.

Silent Sam din't live here. He'd just appear in town one day quiet as a cat, stay a few days and then move on agin, quiet as a cat. Never said much nor did much anybody knowed of. That's why we called him Silent Sam. Usual he'd be riding his nice mount. He had this real nice piece of horse flesh and he were proud as a peacock of it. Couple o'times he were on a non-descript old nag. Don't rightly know why, but I never seed him with any of them twicet in a row. If he were on his mount, he'd be in a nice saddle, too. It were light-brown and tooled real nice all 'round. The pommel, the horn, the cantle and them flaps all had purty flowers tooled in. They was them range flowers and leaves, lotsa leaves all over that saddle. Don't know the proper name of them flowers, but they was purty.

He always had a leather pouch what was on a long leather strap slung 'round his neck and hangin' down his left side. It was always that way. It were tooled too, with a big "S" on the flap o'it, in the middle. He kep' it on all the time, never varied on that. He always wore this wide brim hat. It usual hung on his back from that leather thong it had on it. He had a set o' saddle bags, too, that held the few small things he owned. They was tooled too with a big "S" on each o'em and lots o'other toolins.

3

That horse o'hizzen were the purtiest horse I ever seed. There weren't a mark in that brown coat o'hizzen 'septin that white star on his fore-head. His mane and tail were as black as a midnight in a rain storm. Sam kep' that horse better'n Maw kep' her prize cat and that's sayin' a lot. He curried that horse ever night afor he went t'bed, he did. Cleaned and trimmed them hooves like he were goin' to a horse show or sumthin'. 'Twer a pleasure t'see.

He was kinda like a drifter, he were. He were never no trouble to nobody, just sorta peculiar. Heard some folks say he din't appear t'have all his senses about him. Well now, mabe he din't, come to think on it. He weren't a tall man. If he topped five six that'd be all. His face were round like and he had this unruly mop o'black hair. Don't think he could ever grow a beard, his face were smooth like. And his eyes was close t'gether. One eye, his right one, looked straight and t'other, his left, was lookin' alittle off t'the side. A feller never quite knowed was he lookin' at ya or off somwheres. Because of that all kinds of stories begun to float around about him and his person. To some he was a shady character and they wouldn't have nothin' t'do with him. Some storekeepers and other businesses wouldn't have nothing to do with him neither. They was sure he were goin' t'be stealin' somthin' or t'other. So they'd shuffle him out'n the door soon's he comed in. He soon learnt where he were welcome and where he warn't. Sam never put up no fuss about it, jest din't go back there. But nobody, I mean nobody, had any proof for their wrongheadedness. Sam weren't no trouble ever t'no body.

As a kid I admired him. Oh, it all but skipped my mind t'tell ya m'name. I'm Sonny Kranz. Got called Sonny 'cause I got the same name's my Paw. He's Gresham Potter Kranz II. That makes me Gresham Potter Kranz III.

Well, let me get on wi'm story. But I should say m'Paw's a gud man, too. I admire him most of all, I do.

Well, anyhows … To me there were more to Sam than what a feller first saw. But I thought he were a good man right from the start. Bit peculiar, but a good man. 'Course I were only 'bout twelve year old at the time. He usually come around of an evnin' or early mornin'. You'd just hear of his being in town. He were about twenty or so to hear folks tell it when he first lit into town. I wisht I could have got to know him personal like. But being so much older'and me, it warn't really goin' t'happen, I guess. Still, I wisht it though.

Another thing about Sam was he were smart in his own way. 'Cause he were so short he wasn't able to get into his saddle by hisself from the ground. He had him a piece o'rope tied t'the horn o' his saddle. It had a couple o'knots in it spaced apart. He'd grab one o'them knots and hop up, stick the toe o'his boot in that stirrup and swing into his saddle quick as flippin' a hat on yer head.

He were strong, too, for his size. He could throw that saddle on his horse and cinch it up quick as any man could.

Maw and me was in the general store one time. I were fourteen or so. Maw bought a hunnerd pound sack o'flour. Sam he grabs that sack, heaves it onto his shoulder and carries it outside and throws it on the back o'the wagon Maw and me was in town with. Made me go bug-eyed, it did.

Whenever he left, the whole area would be buzzin' like a buncha bumble bees on a clover field with stories about him. Most of it were about poker. He were one of the best poker players any of us ever seen. When he come, they'd get up a game at Annie Catherine's saloon just t'watch him play. He'd get his hand and then set and watch the cards of the other players. He'd just stare at them cards as if he could look straight through 'em and see what they was. Some players got so uptight about it they'd hold their other hand over the back o'their cards as if they could keep them more secrut that way. But it never hepped; he had some kinda sixth sense about playin' cards. He might lose a hand or two at first, but then he would start to win.

One thing though, if he were losing, he'd quit when he lost all the money he put on the table. But that was real rare like. He 'most never lost. They never played for a lot of money. It was nickels and dimes, sometimes twobit pieces. So nobody resented what he won. He would take his winnings and just disappear into the night without a word. He would never take collateral.

If he won anythin' besides money, he'd always leave it on the table when he left. When he left, nobody ever tried to foller him that I know of. Because he were so silent most everbody just let him to hisself. I think that's the way he wanted it and everybody knowed it.

Another thin y'need t'know is Silent Sam never and I means never drunk a'drop o'likker. He'd drink coffee by the jug full, but never likker.

2 SAM'S NAME AND SUCH

NOW WHY DID we call him Silent Sam, you're wonderin? Well, in these parts, which is Oneida, Texas, we knowed him as Sam Lintz or Landtz or Lits; nobody knowed for sure, nor did we really know where the name come from. But, it seemed natural to call him Silent Sam for his name and for his silent ways.

Now Silent Sam was the nemesis of the local sheriff, who liked to be called Two Gun Taylor. He always wore two pistols. Now Two Gun was a proud man. He were way too big for his briches. He fancied hisself the best detective and tracker there ever was. Truth was he warn't worth a wood nickle. Silent Sam seemed to pleasure hisself in poking holes in Two Gun's high falutin' manner.

One time there was a big ruckus in Mrs. Dory's hen house. Ma Dory, as we called her, was a widow who made a bit of money selling eggs and chickens plucked and ready for the cookin' pot. Well, late one evenin' just after sundown a local lad come runnin' up to the sheriff aclaimin' he seed Silent Sam in Ma Dory's chicken coop. Least ways there was a heap o' cacklin' and noise in that hen house to make a body wonder what were goin' on. So Two Gun jump on his horse and gallops off to that hen house. He sure wanted t'catch Silent Sam in the act. It were dark by this time with no moon out. He crept up near the hen house quiet like with both guns drawn. Couldn't see a thing, he couldn't. Just then he heard a couple three thuds off t'his right. Without thinking Two Gun fired off both guns in the direction of them thuds. Din't hit nuthin' 'sept open air 'tween here and no wheres. It scared them hens so bad they were off they feed and layin' for days.

Silent Sam he come walkin' round the corner o'that coop carryin' a dead 'coon by the tail in one hand and a dead chicken in the other, dropped 'em at the sheriff's feet and walked away. When Two Gun finally got back to his office after talkin to Ma Dory, Silent Sam was asitting in his chair. Two Gun were livid.

Silent Sam said, "Just mindin' the store", then got up and left. Folks said they seed a light on in his rooms back of Sheriff's office all night. Two Gun could stay mad for a week when he got upset.

Later, so the story goes, there were two chickens on the back stoop of a local family that just lost a baby. The story was Sam stole the chickens from Ma Dory after he left the sheriff's office. Don't know if anybody really believed it or not.

Two Gun fancied hisself a good poker player, too. He tried and tried to beat Silent Sam but he never did. They was other little ways that Silent Sam would pester Two Gun.

One evenin' the sheriff and a couple of local boys was goin' to try to see who could outdraw the other in shooting cans off a fence post. They were jest outside of town in a pasture. Two Gun was standin' there with his elbow stickin' way out and his hands hangin down, flexin' his fingers waitin' for the signal to draw and shoot.

Now you need t'member Sam were not very tall. Well, he crept up real bent over and quiet like behind Two Gun, squatted down like, grabbed the gun out of Two Gun's right holster while peekin' under Two Gun's arm and shot that can right off that post and put another hole in it as it flew up in the air afor that darn can hit the ground. Then he quick plopped that gun back in Two Gun's holster afor Two Gun could turn around. It all happened in the blink of an eye, so dern fast you din't know if you really seen it or not. Then Silent Sam just stood there lookin' innocent as could be.

Needless to say, our eyes was like saucers at first. Our respect for Silent Sam went as high as the bell on the school house. Then we all started hootin' and hollerin', it were so funny. But Two Gun got red as them red flannel underwears in the local mercantile, them veins in his neck stuck out like ropes, his cheeks was puffed way out and his eyes was all squinty like and he stomp off. We didn't know Silent Sam could shoot; he never even carried a gun what we knowed of.

3 SAM'S LAST VISIT

SILENT SAM was gone a long time, now. Everybody was itchin' for a good game of poker with him. The men'd sit in Annie Catherine's of'n evenin' a'sippin beer like they was waitin' for a late stagecoach. They were a lotta talk about war in them days. It were over the slave thing. Din't nobody 'round Oneida have slaves that I knowed of. But they were a lotta talk back and forth on it. Couldn't nobody see cause for war on it though. There were some talk 'bout States rights. If y'give ever State its own right t'have or not have slaves, din't 'pear t'most folks would it work. Never did settle anything and talk on it was growing stronger.

Then one day he were back, just like that. Silent as always. When he come back they started up a game. I was goin' on to twenty-two at the time. Silent Sam were winning all night. There was a fair bit of money in the game that night. Finally, it come down to Two Gun, Silent Sam and one other local yokel.

Sheriff had a good hand and were sure he were goin t'win. He called it, but when they laid down their hands Silent Sam won again. Two Gun he jump up and shouted, "You cheated," drew his gun and shot Silent Sam right through the chest.

Silent Sam flew backward with the force of that shot and landed backards on his chair and then went sprawlin' alongst the floor, blood streakin' behin' wherst he slid.

We all stood there like we was froze, shocked outta our minds. We couldn't believe what jest happened. Two Gun were always allowed to keep his guns 'cause he were sheriff. But Silent Sam never cheated. Never. A man ran for Doc Harmon but we could see Silent Sam warn't goin t'make it. He were bleedin' real, real bad.

He sez in a small rattley voice, "Miss Annie Catherine. Miss Annie Catherine."

Annie owned the bar where we was playing. Annie took to Silent Sam right from the start of his comin' to town. She treated him like the best friend she had. She always rustled up something special for Silent Sam when he come. She let him stay in one of her rooms, too, when he wanted to. Never let him pay a red cent for it neither, she din't. She made over him like a maw makes over her only boy child. She were old enough to be his maw.

When he called for her, we said, "She's right here."

He held out his hand a little. She took it. She were cryin' like a baby. Then he said, "What's left of mine is yourn." His last breath just sagged out o' him and that were the end. It were just too sad for words. We was all cryin', truth be told.

By the time we come to our senses and looked for Two Gun he were gone. Gone and clear out of town. Just then Doc come in. He looked at Sam and just shook his head and sed he'd get the undertaker out. Annie Catherine went over to Sam and gentle like took that pouch off'n his shoulder. We told her to look in it to see what was what.

When she did her eyes went open real big. Why, I don't know but she give that pouch t' me. I looked in and to my surprise I seen a gun. I took it out and everyone else was just as shocked. It weren't loaded, but there was bullets with it. There was a rod, a little oil can all wrapped up in a rag to clean the gun.

There was two gold rings tied up in a Bull Durham bag, and a nice Barlow pocket knife, a couple of whittled birds and a dried up willow whistle. One of them rings was big and one was little. No wonder he kep' that pouch so close to him all the time. It were with him when he slep' even.

Annie Catherine tried to give us our money back, but none of us would have it. It belonged to Silent Sam and he give it t' her. We all knowed she needed it real bad. She spent everything she had caring for her sick pa and a no-count brother. After her pa died her no-count brother got hisself shot tryin' to rob a bank. It were good riddance as far as we was concerned. But Annie Catherine took it real hard. Now we was all glad Sam said what he did. Now Annie Catherine had a fair bit more to carry her for a while along with her earnings at the bar.

The horse Silent Sam had this time were his good horse. He had a lot of life left in him. In Silent Sam's saddle bags we found another wad of cash. The horse and the cash went to Annie Catherine, too, of course. All she could do was cry, so we jest put everthin' on the bar. Not one of us could have been happier for Annie Catherine. She deserved ever bit o'it. We all loved that gal, ever one of us. But we was sad about Sam. He din't deserve what Two Gun did t'him.

But it was the way that Silent Sam said, "What's left of mine is yourn," that perked up my ears good. It seemed to me there was more to that story. It made me think of what he left at that grieving family's house. I found out one day those warn't chickens at all, they was pheasants he put on that stoop.

Then there was this young widow near town who lost her husband to some strange sickness, had two young'uns, and was near to losin' her farm. Somebody left her enough cash at her door for her to keep her life together. She never knowed where that cash come from.

She hired a man to hep her with her work around the place. Some men harvested her crop free of charge. She made out real good like. It were a good crop year for all them farmers. After her crop was in she sold her place for a right good profit and then moved back east to her kinfolks.

I think I know who gave her that money. Did wonder me, though, how he came by all that cash. Guess it's no o'my bizness, but it did wonder me.

4 GONE SNOOPIN'

I WERE MIGHTY sure they must be other stories like those around, what I mentioned. Silent Sam was in our town only part of the time. He didn't live here with us. If he was doing things like that by us, I had me a notion he'd been doin' things in other places, too. I decides I had t'find out what I could about him and what he did. What I did find out surprised me a whole lot and at the same time at first made the mystery about him deeper. I could tell lots of stories, but they wouldn't be no point. Besides it would just stretch out the story way too long. I'll just tell what I think are the most important parts.

It were about three weeks afor I could make it to leave. Paw was all for the idea. So I went to town and told Annie Catherine what I was afixin to do. She took to the idea real quick like. She said it made sense for me to take Silent Sam's horse. She finally convinced me t'take it. She give me Sam's pouch, too, with all the stuff that was in it. Said it might mean somethin', she didn't know, I should just take it. And it just might come in handy, special them saddle bags. They were alotta suger cubes in 'em. Were for that horse we reckoned. So I took it all.

When I lit out I took the trail southwest first off. It seemed to make the most sense. That were the way Sam come from. As I rode it came to my mind that it might be a good idea to try to put myself in Silent Sam's place, to try to think like he did. So, I let that horse have his head. That horse just seemed comfortable to keep goin' down the trail we was on. He never even lookt down the side trails. He were sure a nice horse t'ride. Had a real nice pace. Made ridin easy like. Toward the end of the day I decides t' look for a place to bed down for the night. Then that there horse stopped right by a little side trail that went off t'the right. You could hardly see it. I were surprised like, but I spurred that horse alittle and he took on up that side trail.

The trail went up over a rise and then down. It led into a place full of huge rocks, some bigger'n a man, with some hills up behind 'em. That horse wound on through them rocks on a path, some places was just wide enough for my horse and me to get through. We come up on a little cabin t'my surprise. It were more like a shack than a cabin, to be honest. I left the reins on the horse's neck just the way I seen Silent Sam did. He never tied his horse up. I did take his saddle off, though.

No one was in the shack that I could tell, so I walked in. It was creepy; like someone walkin' their fingers up yer back when ya didn't even know they was there. I felt Silent Sam all over this here place. It were simple just like him. And Silent just like him. It were small but had everthing you'd need to be comfortable. I soon had me a nice fire in the fire pit, found some beans I could cook and a pan hanging on the wall. There was even some water in a pail. Some dried meat hung from one of them pole rafters. I couldn't ask for more. There was even a straw tick off on one side with a folded blanket, too, where I could sleep. Slept real good. Nary a dream what I remember.

Woke up afor the sun come up. I went and found the horse a little farther up the trail grazing in some scrub grass. There was a nice stream of water runnin' out of the hills, plenty enough to get a good drink and to wash up a little. I filled my canteen, saddled up the horse and rode out. I gave the horse his head again when we got to the trail. He headed on down just like we was doing yestyday.

That evnin' the sun was purty far in the west when we come to a dusty little settlement. That horse kep' goin' like he knowed where t'go and stopped at one of the bigger houses that had a few trees out front and just stood there under a tree. He bobbed his head up and down acuple o'times and snorted loud like. I had no idea what to do so I just set there awhile. Not too long a man come out of the house, stood there on the verandy and looked at me him chawin' his t'bacy.

After a bit he askt, "That yer horse?"

"Well yes and no, I reckon."

He kep' chawin' a minit, spit off to the side of the verandy and sez, "Maybe ya might want to 'splain yersef."

"Well, afor I do, seems like you know this here horse. Maybe you tell your part and I'll fill in what I know. I've come alookin' for what people might know about the man who owned this here horse."

He chawed some more and spit agin, "You say 'owned' like he don't no more."

"Nope. Reason is he's dead now."

The man just stood there chawin' and shook his head real sad like and he spit again. Then he sez, "Heared he got hissef shot, but din't know were it true or not. Had to be an accident way I reckon. Nobody I know would'a shot him. No reason to."

So I told him the story. He just stood there shakin' his head, sad like.

He put me up for the night in his house. I preferred to sleep in his barn and told him so but he wouldn't have none of it, his missus neither. She had a good feed for us that night and give me a good breakfast next mornin' and some grub for the road.

I took my leave of her and went out on the verandy. The man had brought out my horse all saddled and ready to ride. There was a big gunny sack of hay tied behind the saddle. I could smell it were nice clover hay. He told me to come back t'his place when I was ready, he'd put me up. Ya don't say thankee t'a man like that. Ya jest look at the bag and then nod at him and he nods back.

I felt like I was comin' to the end of this trail 'cause I din' learn nothin' much, but it felt too empty to quit, too. Still I didn't know what to do next. But the answer come soon enough. I was astandin' with one foot in the stirrup and my hand on the saddle horn ready to swing up, when the man sez:

"Silent Sam, as you call him, usual come out of the west when he come this away." That were all. Not a man o'many words, he weren't.

So I mounted up, nodded t' the man, spurred that horse gentle like and give him his head. He went back to the trail we was on and headed west without me doin' nothin'. Soon as we was on the trail he started on a trot. Kept that trot up all mornin'. About noon we come to another dusty little town. But I gotta stop.

This here story's gittin' too long. I can shorten up a whole lot by sayin' everwhere that horse took me it were the same. I din't learn much new about Sam. It was most the same as it was back home.

5 MORE OF THE STORY

THEN ONE DAY, I was a far piece from home by now, I figgered I warn't goin' to learn much more so I just as well set out for home. I was in a place they called Panhandle. So I decides t'get me a drink afor I sets out. I got me a whiskey in the saloon and went and set down by a table to drink it. A man comes up and askt could he sit.

"Din't buy the chairs. Just got me a drink is all."

That seemed good enough for him, so he turns a chair 'round and set backerds on it 'cross from me.

After while he sez, "Hear you been askin' about Sam. Mabe you'all will tell me why."

"Yup." So I told him my story about Sam.

"Heard he got shot. Ah see you got his horse and pouch." So I told him about Annie Catherine and what Sam said. "Well, now, I ain't bein' nosey or nuthin'. You look sotra sad like, like you come to the end of yer trail and would like to know more."

Well, he coulda sed that in the first place, was my thinkin'.

"You knowed him, did ya?"

"Yup."

"Say, you the sheriff hereabouts or sumpthin'?"

'Yup. If ya want to know more you'll haveta go southeast to a place called Claude. There's a doctor there what might know somethin', if anybody does. He getting' up in years but still got a good mind. You go talk to him. Everbody calls him Doc Twofeathers. And one thing. Glad yer doin' what y'are for Sam. He were a good man."

With that he got up and left. I finished my drink and went up to pay. The barkeep wouldn't take my money.

"Anybody doin' a good thing for Sam don't owe nuthin' here. Y'all jus' come on back agin."

Now this here is a right friendly town. I'll be back for sure.

With that news and the way I were afeelin', there was no way I were goin' to sleep atall. 'Sides, I knowed that horse'd know the

17

way. So I saddled up agin and set out. It turned out to be a clear moonlight night. Could see real good. Great for ridin' along. A tune come to mind that my Maw always sung of an evenin':

Abide with me fast falls the eventide,
The darkness deepens, Lord, with me abide.
When other helpers fail and comforts flee,
Help of the helpless, O abide with me.

It seemed to make sense, it did. I was feelin' helpless 'til a couple hour or so ago. But now things was achangin'. Thought come to mind the Good Lord liked what I was doin', too. Made me feel real good, it did.

That horse kep' movin' along the trail. He'd trot down the slopes but he kep' up a good step on the inclines, too. He sensed where we was a'goin', I'm sure. Along about midnight, near as I could tell, we come up on top of a rise. The trail down looked a bit steep, but I could make out it snaked along on down which took most of the steepness out of the ride. Off in the distance about a mile or so from where the trail leveled off I could make out the outline of a town. That horse jogged all the way down and lit into a slow gallop the rest of the way. I knowed for sure we was comin' up on Claude.

Sure enough, he pulled up right by the livery stable in town. I opened the door and that horse pushed right on by me and went in first. Made me smile. He were home. The moonlight came in through a cupola up on the roof and give enough light to see here inside. I took his saddle off but afor I could do the bridle he marched right into an empty stall and starts chompin' on the hay. Yep, he were home. I went over and took the bridle off. He snorted and bobbed his head up and down which I took for thanks. I give him some of them shugey cubes Sam kep' in the saddle bags. That horse rubbed his nose up and down my cheek and chest; made tears come in my eyes. Was glad it were night and I were inside alone.

I took the blanket from behind the saddle, rolled it 'round me and lay down on the pile of hay that was there. Next thing I knowed somebody were shakin' me. Din't even know I fell asleep. I felt good. But then I come full awake and remembered where I was. A boy were asktin me sumpthin'.

Finally I got full awake. I guess I looked up sorta dumb like. He sez to me, "Ah axed y'all whut y'all's doin' heah?"

"I were sleepin' I reckon."

"I knows that. That thar hoss is Mista Sam's hoss. Saw you layin' heah and thot y'all was Mista Sam. But Ah seed y'warn't so Ah went and told M'boss and he wants to know what y'all is doin' heah with Mista Sam's hoss, bein ya ain't Mista Sam."

"No I reckon I ain't. But if'n you take me to yer boss, I'll tell him why I'm here."

"Then y'all betta come wif me direcly."

6 A DISCOVERY

WELL, AGIN I gotta shorten this here story up a little. Went to The Boss and told my story. He sent me to Doc Trueblood, also known as Two Feathers. Must be the doc that sheriff were tellin' me about. So I went and found Doc up behind his house in his garden, just as The Boss said I would.

Doc were a big man. He were more than six foot tall. I could look him straight in the eye. Musta weighed about two forty. Anybody could see he was part Injun. He had a long face with a big flat nose and high cheekbones. He looked like he could outfight any man what took him on. Still he had the look o' somebody who wouldn't hurt a fly without cause.

I told him why I were there. Told him the whole story.

"Son,' he said, "you come with me. You look as if you need some breakfast. The Missus will be happy to fill you up. When you're finished she'll show you into my office."

He talked like no one I'd ever heared afor. Thought it must be from the schoolin' he done to be a doctor. I just stood there dumb like. He looked at me with a big grin and sez, "Well, come then. I'm not going to bite you."

Soon's you saw his Missus you couldn't help but see her eyes. They was laughing eyes. Real purty like. Made you feel at home and yet wonderin' if she seed straight through a body. But she set me down and put a plate afront 'o me. It were soon full of grub like I'd never seed afor.

That were a brekfast t'be remembered. There was corn bread and surp like I never had it. Them sausages was fit for the guvner, with gravy on them biskits that made 'em slide down without hardly takin' a swaller. Never tasted coffee like that coffee. Drank three cups.

When I couldn't eat another bite or take another sip I was showed into Doc's office.

I saw right off why he were called Two Feathers. On his desk was two purty ink pots with printin' on 'em and big feather quills in 'em stickin' up in the air. He saw me lookin' at 'em.

"Those were a gift from the State Governor for the work I did for the State," he sez, noddin' at them quills.

I nodded. I din't know what t'say so I kep m'mouth shut.

The he sez, "You want to know about Sam, I understand. Right?" I nodded agin feelin' a little sheepish. "Then let me tell you. You deserve to know it all. I'll start back a ways.

"Years ago there were two young ladies who moved into this area from Kansas. Their names were Angela Katrina and Liza Beth Barton. They were about 20 and 18, Angela being the oldest. In time they married brothers. Angela married Reuben Levi Langhorn and Liza Beth married his younger brother Samuel Aaron.

"Both families were from solid religious stock. They were regulars at the church meetings except for Samuel.

"The sisters had money at their disposal from the estate of their grandfather, so neither of them was forced to work for a living. The brothers weren't poor either. Rooster, Rueben that is, was a hard worker. He was an excellent carpenter. In fact he built a medical building for me. He told the town council he would donate the labor if the town would furnish the materials, which they gladly did. Angela donated her time in my office at first. She and Rooster weren't able to have children, though she loved them and they took well to her.

"Samuel, on the other hand, I'm sad to say was as worthless as they come. He wasted most of his money and was cruel to Liza Beth. Liza Beth was a kind and generous person. She was excellent at teaching and donated her time teaching at the local school. She did all the work involved for teaching there in her schoolroom. We all knew it was to stay away from Samuel as much as possible.

"Still, after a few years she became pregnant. While she was carrying her child it became clear she was ill with consumption. It became apparent that because of her weak lungs she should never have become pregnant. She went into labor in a badly weakened condition. I have never known a woman to have such a difficult time as she had. She was in labor for days.

"I knew she couldn't live and spoke of that to her. She knew even before I told her. I wanted to perform an operation to remove the child, but she would have none of it. She was certain that would kill the child, too. I couldn't change her mind.

Finally, the child was far enough along for me to help its birth. Liza Beth died before the child was fully born. Samuel was, of course, nowhere around. In fact, he skipped town and didn't even attend the funeral. It came out Liza Beth had a premonition of her death. When she first became ill she willed the remainder of her estate to her sister to care for her child.

"Samuel was fit to be tied when he found out, but I told him if I ever got wind of him laying a hand on his wife again, I would see him hanged. As far as I know, he never did. Though, he didn't do anything else, either.

"It seemed only natural for Angela to take the baby as her own when her sister died. We both knew from the beginning that the child suffered damage in the birth. It was just too long before he was able to come into the air which he needed to be fully healthy.

"Angela and Rooster loved that child as if he were their own. I don't believe they ever told Sam he was not their natural child. Angela stopped working for me and gave her life for the child, bless her.

"They named him after his father, but God knows that man didn't deserve it. He never, ever inquired after his son's welfare. Angela taught Samuel everything as he grew, though there was much he wasn't able to learn. When he became of school age they sent him to school, but that didn't work out for obvious reasons.

"So, Angela continued to teach him at home. In fact, he learned more than he ever would have any other way. One day there was a deck of cards on the table which weas left from their playing the evening before. Sam pointed to the box they were in and said, 'Twenty-six red and twenty six black,' to Angela's utter amazement.

"Sam had never seen the box before that. She used the cards after that to teach him his numbers and he took to it with no trouble.

"One day she noticed he had the cards neatly arranged according to the four suits. He sat looking puzzled. So she taught him what the various suits were. Soon he wanted to play cards with them. Again, they became amazed with his ability to play poker. He seemed to be able to count the cards, or something. Soon he was always winning. He loved that game. Unfortunately it also became the source of his death as you've told me.

"When Sam was about seventeen or eighteen Rooster developed a severe heart problem. He lingered about six months or so as an invalid and then died. Angela contracted consumption as did Liza Beth and died a little over a year later. It was a good thing she didn't have to work. Her lungs, like her sister's I discovered, were in a very poor condition when she took ill.

"We all wondered how Sam would make it through losing his mother. Rooster's death did not appear to affect him much. He still had his mother. But now, it was a different question. To our surprise at the graveside, Sam moved forward and looked down into the open grave at the coffin below. We all stood holding our breaths. Then he turned around as said loud enough for all of us to hear,

"'Papa went to be by God and be happy. Mama went to be happy with him. Amen!'

"We laughed and cried at the same time. I don't believe I have ever heard a better eulogy than that. We knew Sam would be fine. You've experienced how well he did. And your travels have also confirmed that.

"Well, young man, that's the story of Samuel Aaron Langhorn, Jr. As I said, doing what you are doing, you deserved to hear as much as I've told you. I don't think I've missed anything essential, but if you have a question feel free to ask it. I'm only sorry to hear that he died as he did."

I told him I had no questions. Hearin' the story left me a little winded, it did. I wanted to get out t'get some air and think on what I heard so's I wouldn't go and forget it.

He held up his hand and motioned for me to sit back down. "I almost forgot. I'm sure there is money left over in his account at the bank. I'll take you to the lawyer who is the executor of his estate. I'm sure he'll agree that it was Sam's will that this Annie Catherine should have what's left in his account. We'll go now, if you have nothing else to do? ... No? Then we'll go now. After we'll come back here for something to eat and then you can be on your way or do whatever you deem best."

I was awestruck, as they say. I was glued to that chair. Doc walks up, puts his hand on my shoulder and sez we should be goin'. So I unglued m'self and went with him.

7 A LAWYER AND A BANKER

THE MINIT I walked in that lawyer's place I knowed he was Doc's son. He were built like Doc, his face were the same shape and he had sorta a flat nose, just not as flat as Doc's. But he had his Ma's eyes and her wavy hair and it were black, black as the ace of spades. The way them two greeted made a body know they was right kindly one t'the other.

That lawyer man set me down and heared m'story. All the time he's writin' on his paper and a gal that was there in the room with him at her table was awritin', too. Writin' faster and ever I seed anybody write. Then he pulled some papers from a drawer when I were finished that looked legal like and wrote on them here and there in different places.

Then he stans up and sez, "Well, Mr. Kranz," (aint nobody named me Mr. Kranz b'for). "Mr. Kranz," he sez, "now we need to go to the bank. If you'll come with me..."

With that he marches around his desk and heads for the door. Weren't nuthin' I could do but foller along behind, with Doc close on m' heels.

When we got us to the bank we was led to a side room where there were a man who looked important like in his suit and vest, a white shirt and black bow tie. The door was put shut and we all was set down. There was a lot of talkin' and writin' and such. Most of it I din't rightly understand. But it 'peared they did so I just set there. Then a strange thing happened. They told me the man what was behind that desk were also the local judge.

Well, he stands up and tells me to stand, too, and raise m'right hand, which I did. Then he says we was goin' to take an affedavit, he called it. I was told I had to swear t'the truth, the whole truth, and nuthin' but the truth, s'help me God, which I did. But it made me break out into a sweat, it did and I was shakin'. Never had part of any doin's like this. It were all mighty strange t'me.

I were askt a whole bunch of questions. No need to repeat 'em all 'cause they was about everthin' that happened and what I saw and heard.

'Special about Sam's bein' killed. Y'know 'em all from this here story anyways.

Then they scribbled on a bunch of papers and askt me t' sign a bunch of 'em, too. I were right glad I learnt to read and write so's I could do the signin' and stuff.

Then that lawyer man come over t' me and give me a bunch o' letters. He called 'em onveelopes, but they just looked like normal letters t'me. Well, I could see on two of 'em was Annie Catherine's name and one had my name on it. He told me the fat one for Annie Catherine was papers for her to sign and get back t'him. The other to her was tellin' her what she'd be gittin', five thousand three hunerd dollars from Sam's estate. I 'bout choked up. Annie Catherine was goin' t'have a faint when she heard this.

In that there letter for me was a three hunnert and seventy five dollar, he said. I all but fell off m'chair soon's he sez that. When I could talk agin I tried t'give it back but he wouldn't take it. Sed it were mine for my time and expenses. I were feelin' like I could buy the whole world. I knowed of course I can't but just t'same, I felt like I could. Never had me three hunnert and seventy five raw dollar afor this.

They sed the money for Annie Catherine'd be put in the bank in Onieda and I could tell her it were comin' soon.

When everthin' were over, they sez I can go home, which I really wanted t'do.

I rode three hard days and stopped at only a couple, three places what I 'spected would be best t'drop the story of Sam. Never told nobody about the money, though. Figgered it were m'own busnis, not their'n. I went straight home, o'course. told m' Maw and Paw about everthin' even the money part, too. Maw was acryin' and Paw was lookin' real serious like while I told 'em the story. When I finish Paw he stood up and pulled me t'my feet and gives me a great big hug and then he starts shakin' my hand as if he wanted my arm or sumpthin' and told me how proud he were of me and what I done.

8 BACK HOME

I GOT ME home on a Mundy.

Next day went straight t'Annie Catherine and told her the whole story. Ever little detail. Din't let on about the money though. Wanted that to be a surprise.

She cried most of the time I talked and after she told me, too, how proud she were of what I'd done for Sam. She made me keep that horse for my own. Din't want to a first but she made me see the sense o'it. So I got me one fine horse, t'boot. Life right now is purty good, I figger.

Got some more t'tell but this here story is getting' lot longer'n I figgered so I'm goin' to stop and go back make me some chapter headin's the way they is in real books and such. So that's why y'll be able t'see the different parts now. I rekkin I'll be needin' some help t'do it. That school marm'll help, I'm athinkin'.

I'm back now and I'll try t'finish up this here story. That school marm was right keen t'help me. She said I have a right good story. She were proud t'help me. Them headins looks real good t'me, too. 'Course, she scribbled them in the margins 'n such, with arrows pointin' t'where they need to be. Well, that school marm sed she'd be right glad t'type it up when I'm done with it. I'm athinkin' I'll have her do just that. Nice lady, she is.

Back to'm story.

Well, I gets me t'the bank and with the help o'that banker I put my money in an account as he called it. Told me I'd be gettin' interest, as he called it. But I figger I got a lot o'interest in it aready. I can put more in if I like or I can take it out and use it, if I want to. I 'spose it'll be safe in there. Guess I gotta trust him.

Well, the wemin folks decides they's goin' t'put on a big do down t'Annie Catherine's come Satyday. Ma let out that there's goin' t'be sumpthin' big 'bout noon for Annie Catherine. Everbody can come, just bring along sumthin' t'eat, reglar stuff or pies and such, don't matter. Just come an' take whats you want to share with the rest.

Come Satyday I never seen so many people. Word got out and it look s'if the whole state come out. We rustled up a bunch o'wood horses and planks t'set all the eats on out in front o'Annie Catherine's. Weren't room enuf inside. Everbody was talkin' and eatin' and havin' a good time. Good thing it were a nice day.

Long 'bout noon Ma sez for me t'get up on the verandy and make my speech to Annie Catherine which I was just about t'do.

I get's me up and sed as loud as I could so's everbody could hear purty good about what I done and what I found out about Sam down in Claude. I told 'em I were writin' the story up and when it were done I might have it printed in the newspaper so's anybody who wanted to could read it.

Then I called Annie Catherine up on the verandy. I told Doc afor the affair what I was afixin' t'do and he knowed he needed to be on hand. My Paw was there too. When she come up I sez t'her there was more to the story that I told her that I din't tell her yet. I had Sam's pouch on and reached into it and pulls out them two letters, what that lawyer called onveelopes. I sez t'her the big fat letter had some papers in she needed t'sign 'n get back t'the lawyer in Claude. The other letter, the little one, would tell her sumptin'. Accordin' t'that lawyer I was t'ask her t'open it and give it t'me t'read, which I did. She opened it up and give me the paper inside. There were such a hush come over that crowd of people what you'd think everone of 'em had dropped dead on the spot. They was so quite like, but they was all eyes and ears. I unfolded that letter. On the top was some pichers and fancy writin' and such.

Then come the rest. This is what it read:

TO WHOM IT MAY CONCERN:

This instrument is a legal and authoritative declaration of the following:

BE IT RESOLVED that according to the sworn testimony of one Gresham Potter Kranz III of Oneida, Texas, one Samuel Aaron Langhorn II did on his death bed verbally and audibly express his last will and testament as to the disposition of his estate.

BE IT FURTHER RESOLVED that according to said sworn testimony the decedent did verbally and audibly before his demise name and designate the sole heir of said estate.

BE IT FURTHER RESOLVED that, according to said sworn testimony, Miss Annie Catherine Marshall of Oneida, Texas was designated and named as sole heir of the estate of the decedent, Samuel Aaron Langhorn II.

BE IT FURTHER RESOLVED that after all justifiable State, Local and other legal expenses have been fully paid and satisfied the remaining estate totals five thousand three hundred dollars and seventy-three cents ($5,300.73),

BE IT FURTHER RESOLVED that said amount will be forthwith deposited in the Oneida Bank in Oneida, Texas payable on request to aforementioned Miss Annie Catherine Marshall.

BE IT FURTHER RESOLVED that when said Miss Annie Catherine Marshall shall have requested transfer of said monies to her account or withdrawn them in cash or in any other way disposed of said monies, the last will and testament of said Samuel Aaron Langhorn II shall be deemed fully executed.

In testimony of the authenticity of these proceedings the seal of the State of Texas has been affixed and imprinted.

On the bottom of that there letter there was a lot of other writin' that looked legal like, so I din't read that. Din't read the signatures neither.

Annie Catherine fainted dead away when she heard the amount of money she was goin' t'get, just like I thought. That's why I had Paw and Doc on hand. They laid her on the lounge swing on the verandy and Doc used some smellin' salts t'bring her 'round again.

When she did she kep' sayin', "Lord, Lord, what did I do to deserve this?"

First it started slow like. Then it begun t'get louder and louder. There was clappin', then hollerin', then the whole crowd was screamin' and dancin' in the street. You'd a thunk the President just walked into town and give everbody a million dollar.

Then that crowd started shoutin' all together, "Miss Annie

Catherine, Miss Annie Catherine." It finally died down and everbody went back to eatin' 'n dancin' 'n havin' a good time.

9 SOMETHING UNEXPECTED

AFTER I GIVE that speech I wanted to be alone a little. I hadn't et yet 'cause I were a little nervy about the speech. So I went inside. There was plenty t'eat inside, too, so I filled up a plate, got me some coffee and set down by a table. The place were practical empty, it were. I were enjoyin' the grub when in walks Mabel Custis. Her first name is actual Jennie, but everone calls her Mabel. It's what she prefers. Don't know why.

Mabel's a few year younger'n me. Was in school when I were there, too. She were a smart one, she were. Sharp as they come. She'd always get the best grades of us all. She's sure purty, she is. She got long sorta brown hair with natural curls aplenty and them nice brown eyes makes a feller look twicet at her, if y'dare. Nice ladylike figger she's got. She's taller'n lotta girls and slim and trim, as they say. She gotta be five nine, five ten, thereabouts. Always dresses nice and lady like. She's one that'd look good in just 'bout anything.

She's not much shy 'round men folks neither. When we was in school, she played ball with us boys. We always liked to have her 'cause she could hit a ball and run a base with the best of us and her in skirts. I 'member one guy thought he could get sorta fresh with her. He learnt his lesson real good. She set him on his backsides literal, she did. What a punch she give him!

We din't know what he did, but she punched him in the nose hard enought t'make it bleed. Then she screams at him, "You ever do anything like that again, and I'll lay you out for a week. Do you hear me?" Then she kicked some dirt at him and walked away. She were real disgusted we could tell. Made us all take notice, it did.

Near as I can recall, that guy lef' school and we never heard from him agin. He were a bad one anyways and we all thought it were good riddance of bad rubbish, as they say. We knowed she could keep her word and we respected her. I always thought she were the purtyest girl I ever seen but it din't much go futher n'that. If I had thought on it, I woulda thunk she'd want a different man from me.

Well, Mabel comes across the room and pulls out a chair and sits down purty like across from me. She set her elbows on the table, laced her fingers and put her chin on top'o 'em. I were surprised, I were. Almost made a swaller cetch in m'throat.

"Sonny…," she sez, "No, it isn't Sonny anymore to me. It's Gresham Potter. Gresham Potter, I think you are the bravest man I know," she sez with that purty smile on her face. "Now, I can see you want to make light of it, so don't say anything right now. I mean what I said. No one would have done what you did. And you did everything just right today, too. You did a good thing for Sam and for Miss Annie, as it turns out. I just wanted to tell you how I feel."

I tried my best t'thank her for her kindly thoughts but it come out kinda mixed up. I don't even want to write down what I sed.

Mabel just smiled. Then she stood up to go but turns around and sez, "Don't make yourself such a stranger around our house."

They ain't no lightnin' 'n thunder bolt coulda hit me harder'n that. The lightnin' was goin' up and down m'back had me stuck on that chair tighter'n any glue or bolts coulda done. My appetite was gone, it was. I couldn't have swallered another bite iff'n my life depended on it. She were askin' me t'come callin' on her, she was. My mind were a goin' fifty ways at oncet. I was goin' t'have to talk to Maw about this in privet like, I was. Mabel's words was one thing I never 'spected. Maw'd hep know m'mind.

When I talked to Maw she sez, "'Pears to me you knows what y're fixin' to do, y're just skeered to do it is all. Shucks bein' skeered never killed a body. It just makes ya keep yer mind so ya don't go doin' some fool thing and make an ass of yerself. If ya won't do a thing 'cause yer skeered, where ya get in life?"

See, that's the way Maw is. She don't give no answers, she jus' makes a feller think straight. So I called at Mabel's house. And t'make a long story short, we got on real gud, and she said she hoped I'd call agin real soon. Reckon I'll do jus' that. I can't stop now and don't want to neither.

10 SOMETHING UNUSUAL

SO LIFE WENT on a week or two, maybe three. Then one day I was workin' on the fence way back on our place. Paw was gone for the day. About supper time he comes home and helps me with the chores around the barn and such. We was jus' done when Maw called for supper.

We et. Paw din't get up like usual and Maw stayed sittin', too. Then Paw looks at me and sez, "Son, a bunch of us men had us a meetin' in town t'day 'cause we need a new sheriff for our area. We come to a decision and made us an election. In short we decided us that you should be our new sheriff."

Well bowl me over with a feather, will ya. Me? A sheriff? Somebody's wrongheaded.

But I sed out loud, "Yer wantin' to tell me what the joke is, I reckon."

"No, Son, there ain't no joke about it. We're serious as serious can be. Yer twenty-six goin' on twenty-seven. With your mind like it is, you need sumthin' bigger'n this farm for yer life. You got the makin's for it. We all know from what you jes' did you got the ability if you got the will.

"There's another decision we made, too. We want you to be a proper sheriff that's been schooled to be one. We all know you can't afford it, and yer Maw and me can't afford it neither, least ways not by ourselves. What we're goin' to do is take us a collection and send you off to school. Word is it'll take six months or so right off and then you could do some more studyin' later like after you've had some 'xperience under yer belt."

Might be he coulda told me in the mornin' so's I had me a day to wrap my mind around it. Maybe coulda got me a night's sleep then. 'Cause Lord knows I sure aint gonna get one t'night.

"'Pears t'me by the look on yer face, yer fixin' t'say No, Son…"

"No Paw. I aint fixin' t'say No and I aint fixin' to say Yes. You just put a purty big pile o' hay on m'fork is all. I don't know yet can I lift it or not. Maybe I needs me sum help. In the end I'll likely be a fool and say 'Yes', but right now I need to do me sum thinkin' on it."

"That's fair 'nuff. Let's leave it like that then for now."

Like I was thinkin', I din't get no sleep. Well somewhere t'ward mornin' I drifted off awhile. Had me a crazy dream about tryn' t'swim and me, I wouldn't even get near the water.

Maw let me sleep and I woke up when I smelt bacon fryin'. Got me out and dressed real quick like and went downstairs. Paw was by the table drinkin' coffee. The way his plate looked he already et.

I was about to 'pologize but he put up his hand and stopped me. "Just eat yer breakfast. Take the day off and don't bother yer head about the farm t'day." Then he got up and went out.

I din't know what t'do. I saddled up and rode into town, but it were too early to go Annie Catherine's. It were just the same for Mabel. Finally, I went down by the river where there's a nice spot to rest under some trees. I laid me down and fell fast asleep. Next thing m'horse were nudgin' me with his nose. Guess he were checkin' were I dead or not. I look up and seen it were about noon. Good time to go to Mabel's place. Give m'horse some of them shugey cubes which he likes real good.

When I gets me t'Mabel's place I told her there was some talkin' I need t'do, can we go to the river. She sez if I can wait she'd pack some grub so's we could eat there while we talk. She's got a right good head on her shoulders, that one does.

So I told her all about what happened yestday and all. Then I sez I had a question t'askt her. She takes m'hand in both of her'n. Din't 'xpect that, I din't. I near about jumped outa my skin. Din't know that's how a woman's hand felt. There was all kinds of prickly feelins' runnin' up and down m'arm and everwhere else, too, I reckon. There were some strange feelin's, but it were good at the same time.

When I could manage it I sez, "Mabel m'question is will you wait for me whilst I do my schoolin', 'cuz that's what I have a mind t'do. It'd sure pleasure me if I knows yer awaitin' for me."

She looks at me with her purty brown eyes and a big grin and sez, "Gresham Potter, are you asking me to wait to get married until you come back from your training?"

I gulped. *I guess that's what I were askin'. I just din't relize it. When I comes to,* I sez, "Yes, ma'am, I reckon that's just what I'm askin'. I guess I'm askin' you t'marry me when I gets back from Fort Worth."

She were cryin'. She leans her head on m'shoulder and sez, "Yes, Gresham Potter, I will be glad to wait for you. And I will be thrilled to become your wife."

I din't know what else t'do so I puts m'arms 'round her and kist her and held her tight like for awhile. Sure din't know this were the way things like this was supposed to feel. Ain't complain' like, just surprised. Come t'think on it, it's real nice, I reckon. Them six months is lookin' a whole lots shorter already.

11 MORE UNUSUALNESS

WHEN I GETS me back home Maw and Paw was real surprised. Least ways Maw acted surprised but I seen in her eyes she warn't. She were real pleased.

Them dinners Mabel and me had down they by t'river after that on Satydays was real nice, they was.

Things was shapin' up for me to get down to Fort Worth for that schoolin'. The banker wrote some letters on it and had it all arranged. I were to leave in a week. Then that Fridy noontime, we was just sittn' down t'dinner when a knock comes on the door. When Paw went t'open it there were a United States Marshall standing there.

Paw askt him in and sez, "This good news or bad?"

"'Spose it's good news, in a way."

"Well, then y'had anythin' t'eat? We's just settin' us down."

"That's right kindly of y'all. Don't mind if I do."

Maw already was getting' a plate and such for him.

Paw sez, "Good. Let's eat then. 'Good news kin wait. Bad news must be told right off."

When we was finished that Marshall looks at me and sez, "You're Gresham Potter Kranz III, I 'spose, ain't cha?"

I nodded m'head, "Yeah, I reckon that's me."

"Well, I got me here a subpoena for you." And he pulls a letter outa a pocket on the inside of his jacket. I guess m'face was a great big question mark. He sez, lookin at me, "A subpoena is a notice for you t'come and testify at a court trial." That question mark didn't go away. He saw it and sez, "Probably should tell y'all what's goin' on.

"Y'see, when y'all came down to Claude about Sam Langhorn, y'all confirmed what we had heard about Sam's being shot and all. Well, there was no way we could let such a thing pass. To make a long story short, we had a man who was involved

39

in various crimes down our way some years ago. But he skipped town before we could bring him in. Word was he'd come up your way. But we heard no more. Your story made us suspect it was the same man what shot Sam. We started looking into it. About that time a Federal Marshall from up Oregon way was transferred to us to fill a vacancy we had. When he heard our story something started clicking for him. A man appeared in their territory who they didn't trust for one reason and another. He suspected it was the same man.

"We sent him and one of our men up there. When our man saw him he spotted him right off for the man that we wanted. He was apprehended and brought down to Texas. He'll be put on jury trial for all those crimes, especially the murder of Samuel. Y'all have to come down to Dallas and tell the jury your story. That boy needs to be put away. If the jury finds him guilty, there is no way the judge will spare his life. He'll be hanged, no question.

"The trial is in three weeks. Soon as you can, you get on down to that Lawyer in Claude. He'll get you ready to testify.

"Good luck, son, y'all will be doing your fellow man a good thing."

We was all dumfounded. It took us awhile to get our minds workin' right agin. Sam was agoin' t'get his justice after all.

He turns t'Maw and sez, "Thank you kindly, Ma'am, for a delicious dinner."

"Any time, yer welcome at m'table."

With that he gits up but before he leaves he turns around and sez, "I almost forgot. I have another letter for you young Gresham." He pulls another letter outa his pocket and hands it to me. "It's some reward money. When we first heard about Sam's being shot a number of men put up a reward for the capture of the murderer. We all agreed you were the rightful owner of the reward. You'll find a little over eight hundred dollars in that envelope. Now I can see you aren't of a mind to accept the money, but it's yours for what you did. Use it as best you can."

I din't know what to do else, so I got up and took it and shook his hand and just nodded to him, 'cause iffen I opened my mouth I would just blubber is all.

After he went I told Paw now I could pay fer my schoolin'. But he said right off that the money was mine to live on. The folks here about needs to have a part in what's goin' on, he sez. They needs to do this. They'd feel like they'd be cut off from somethin' good. They're proud to do what they're doin'.

After we done some more talkin', Maw, Paw and me, I went to the bank and added my eight fifty-three to the hunnert and seventy-five already there. Then I went off to Mabel and then Annie Catherine t'tell 'em about the Sheriff and the reward. After that the story spread fast as a rattle snake can strike, it did. Seems everbody I saw wanted to tell me how proud they was about it. I reckon everbody feels like they're helpin' a little to bring Sam his justice.

There was a lot of good things happenin' t'me in the last whiles and it came t'my mind it were all because of Sam's bein' shot. It din't sit right good in my mind. M'mind was upset like a stomach is when y'et sumthin' bad. Din't seem right, me gettin' good outa a man's death. I'd druther Sam'd be alive than this. It were hard on m'mind and m'feelins, it were. Couldn't get it settled no way I looked on it. When Mabel and me was t'gether she noticed sumpthin' was wrong. So I told her about m'feelins. She sez it might be a good idea to talk to the preacher man what was comin' Sundy to hold a meetin'. Seemed like a good idea. Good woman, that one.

Well Sundy when he come to the part to give his speech, he opened up his bible and read some words that set themselves deep in m'mind. He read *And we know that all things work together for good to them that love God.* He read more but that's what I 'member good.

When he talked he said, "A lot of bad things happen in this old world we live in. But bad things don't stop the Good Lord from doing his good work. He is able to make great blessings come from great tragedy. That does not make the bad a good thing. The bad stays bad, but the Good Lord is so great he can make something good from the bad. It makes the world a little better place to live in. Our part is not to keep our minds on the bad. That would be keeping your mind on the past, which does not help. We need to keep our minds on the future. Those that love the Good Lord will see his hand working to make the world a better place. They must hear the Good Lord's calling to them to take their part and work for good, too."

Well, I may not be sayin' 'xactly what he sez, but near enough. He had m'mind workin' like Maw's churn makin' butter, he did. Din't hear the rest o'what he sed. What I heard were enuf for me. I knowed there is a God. Learnt it in school and from Maw's readin' her bible to us. She always read at Christmas the part of his bein' born and at Good Frydy and Easter Sundy the parts of his bein' killed and risin' agin.

Never thought about lovin' him, but I guess when it come down to it that's what it is. Well, what were happening to me was good comin' outa bad. That churn jest made butter for me. I din't need to talk t'the preacher, he talked to me and set m'mind straight. It were workin proper agin. Sure is better that way. I have to get me one of them Bibles for me and Mabel when we starts our home.

After the meetin' Mabel comes up t'me and afor she could say anthin' I told her what I heard the preacher said t'me. Saw a tear in her eye, I did. Right there outside the meetin' house she stands up on her tippy toes, puts her arms around my neck, pulls my head down and kisses me on the cheek. I 'spose I got purty red.

She looks at me and giggles and sez, "Why Gresham Potter, you're blushing," and giggles some more. I cain't hep that. At the same time I was proud to know her. She shore is a good woman, that one.

Life is real good, I reckon.

When I gets home I was settin' there by Maw's table drinkin' m'coffe whilst she fixed up some dinner. I were thinkin' 'bout that preacher's talk. Sudden like sumpthin' comes to m'mind. I had one more thin' t'do afor I went south.

After dinner m'Paw looks at me like he wants t'talk.

"Kin we talk later, Paw? I got me a visit I gotta make." Him and Maw looks t'each other knowin' like. "No. It ain't that visit, though it were a good idea," I sez. "This here visit ain't to the livin'."

When I come t'Sam's grave I set there a spell not knowin' what t'say. It were sad and happy at the same time, it were. I was glad good was comin' out of bad but iffen I had a choice Sam would be alive.

Finally I sez, "Sam, I hopes y'kin see what's happening down here or else maybe somebody'll tell y'bout it. I come to know you a little, I did. I 'spect y'have a lot better life now. But I wants y't'know the good things about your life are still happening. Guess I'm the one's getting' the best part of that and I wants t'thank you a whole bunch and you go tell the Good Lord how thankful I am. I told him myself too, but twicet won't matter, I 'spect. You were a good man and y'still are, I reckon. The best part fer me right now is yer goin' to get justice after all. You rest easy now, y'hear, and one day we'll meet agin."

POTTER'S TALES

1 GRAM AND GRAND

GRESHAM POTTER KRANZ III was his full name. I happen to be named after him and my father. That makes me GP the V. (I was often called that or just The Fifth) He was my grandfather and I loved him. We called him Grand and grandmother was Gram.

Gram's name was Jennie Custis, but she preferred the name Mabel for some unknown reason. Gram would never say why. All she'd say was 'That's what I prefer.'

Grand and Gram were great together. Gram loved Grand with all her heart and Grand doted on Gram all his life. When Gram found out I wanted to write up some stories about Grand, she was excited. She told me a lot about Grand. He was very shy around women. But he was handsome. Every girl in school wanted to be his heartthrob. Of course, girls didn't let a boy know that in those days.

Well, Gram had her eye on Grand, too. She knew one day she would get an opportunity to wake him up. It came when he came back from finding out about Sam. When he went inside to eat after his talk that day, she knew it was time. Her eyes twinkled when she told me. She told him not to make himself so scarce around their place. She saw the shock she gave Grand. She had to get out or she'd likely spoil it all if she burst out in a giggle.

Grand took the hint, she said.

When Grand came back from the sheriff's school they were married. It took place on the first day of May. The weather was balmy. It was such a great wedding. Everybody from miles around came. It took place on the veranda of the saloon so everyone could see it. Grand wore his sheriff's uniform and Gram was dressed in a pearl white gown. It had forty buttons on the back.

Grand and Gram used to come to our house for Sunday dinner or we would go to their house. Grand was a tall man, at least six foot three. When I was a youngster, five or six years old, I thought he was the tallest man in the world. And he looked old.

As I look back, I realize that was my impression as a child. He didn't look much older to me when they laid him out in the casket.

Grand was a handsome man. Besides being tall he had a square chin and a mop of curly dark brown hair which he kept to the day he died. I say a mop because his hair was unruly. He kept it cut quite short for that reason. He probably weighed well over two hundred pounds, but because of his height he was not fat. In fact, he had little excess fat on him. He was all muscle and strong as an ox. They said he could lift twice his weight with ease. When the men of the area would get together in the saloon on Saturdays, they would try to get Grand to use his strength in some way or another. He usually wouldn't fall for their tricks, but when he did stories of what he did would be told endlessly. And they grew with the telling.

He had dark brown eyes that were nearly the color of his hair. They were laughing eyes. You had the impression that he had just heard a good joke. Another thing that impressed me about Grand was his hands. They were big and strong. He had a grip that would make the strongest of men cringe. And he had arms to match. They were big. The muscles on his forearms and upper arms bulged out. He didn't drink liquor much, but like I said, he could usually be found in the saloon on Saturday. When a stranger came in, the men would often start up arm wrestling. The purpose was to get Grand to wrestle with the stranger. He would start out slow and then force the other man's arm so fast it would nearly throw the guy off his chair.

2 THE SHERIFF

AFTER A LOT of coaxing Grand gave me permission to dig into his records, as he called them. I was surprised that Grand kept records of his human side. I asked him about that. He told me in his characteristic style, "Ah jest wrote down what happened is all. That's jest the way it were."

One of the more humorous ones is a tale about his encounter with a man named Taylor Foxx. Foxx liked to arm wrestle because he was good at it. He could take just about anyone. He wanted to wrestle Grand in the worst way, but Grand always begged off for some reason only he knew.

Then one time Foxx laid down a hundred dollar bill and bet he could beat Grand. Finally, Grand yielded. They sat down and every eye in the saloon was on that table. They chose a ref. Foxx usually won because he was so quick to begin pushing. Grand knew that, of course, and Foxx got Grand's arm over slightly. Grand got his arm straight up with what looked like a great effort. They were that way several minutes. Then Grand said, "This is enought," and pushed the man's arm down with little effort.

Foxx turned red as flannel underwear. He blubbered trying to say Grand cheated. But he knew it was not true. He stomped out of the saloon and never wrestled again that anybody knew. The men said if Foxx wasn't so proud he could have enjoyed the game even though he lost. After all, it was fair and square.

Now, Grand was sheriff around those parts. He had been for years on end. Before Foxx walked out Grand shoved the bill back to him and told him to keep his money. But Foxx just walked away. Grand gave it to Widow Campton who had two young children and was having a hard time. She couldn't believe her eyes. She fainted. Grand called the doc in, who revived her quickly. She tried to pay her bill at the Mercantile, but she was told she owed nothing. Grand got a few people to foot the bill. That's the way Grand was. He was always helping people that needed it.

He got to be sheriff because he solved the murder of a man they called Silent Sam. Grand wrote that up. Actually, he printed the entire story. The original was in Grand's files. After Grand wrote it up, somehow it got out. He thinks someone saw it and talked about it. The local newspaper editor sneaked into Grand's office and stole it, then printed it. Grand wasn't too happy about it. He said he wrote it up for his own benefit, not for anyone else. But he did save a copy of that newspaper article, to my surprise.

Grand liked children and they liked him. They'd gather around his office on nice days if he happened to be in. They'd get him to tell them stories. I think he secretly liked it, but he'd pretend he was busy. They knew he'd come out sooner than later and tell them stories.

This part of Grand's life was common knowledge. Everyone talked about how good Grand was with 'the young 'uns.'

Grand was a religious man. When I say religious I mean that his religion was a part of his life. He was morally upright. He said what he learned from the Bible was the guide of his life. He was honest and fair in all his judgments. Everybody knew he never played favorites and especially he would never take a bribe. There were drifters who learned that the hard way. Try to bribe Grand and you'd end up in jail for a week.

Now, the stories he told the children were often stories from the Bible. He said he knew that would help them to grow up good. They'd be more ready to be better people when they 'growed up.' Some parents didn't like him telling stories from the Bible. His answer was, "Well, then, you'd best keep those younguns of yorn home, I reckon."

Those 'younguns' who did come to listen were a good source for information, Grand found out. They'd tell him things they saw or heard. Grand would thank them and pretend he wasn't all that interested. He said he did this so the children wouldn't start to brag about what they told him.

.

3 A CONFESSION

ONE DAY A BOY of about twelve came to Grand's office. He looked real serious.

"You look mighty serious, young man. You got something on yer mind? Now you jest you speak up. There won't come any harm to it."

After shifting back and forth on his feet, the boy said, "Mr. Sheriff, I won't get into trouble none iffen I tell you somthin', will I?"

"Well, iffen it weren't you doing the thing, of course not."

"Well, I seen somthin a ways back and it's been botherin' me somthin' fierce. And I reckon I need to tell you and get it off my mind."

"Umm hmm." Grand swiveled around on his chair, hooked a chair rung with the toe of his boot, pulled it close, and told the boy to just sit down and speak his mind.

The boy sat down. "Well, you see, Mr. Sheriff, I come in here to use your privy what you got here. I heared somebody come in. I was skeered it was you. I peeked out the door. It weren't you. I seen the man from the newspaper in here. He was lookin' around in your desk. He found what he was lookion' fer. He sez, 'Ah, here it is. I knew I'd find it.' Then he shoved it in his shirt and snuck out the back door. I'm real sorry fer usin' yer privy, but I didn't want to dirty my pants, see. But my maw sed you needed to know what I saw. She sed if you fined me I'd have to work it off somehow."

"But how do I know you didn't find that paper and go give it to the newspaper man, eh?"

That boy wriggled real hard and sat up in the chair, "Oh, no sir, Mr. Sheriff, I'd never steal nuthin'. On my word, I won't steal. Your stories from that Bible made me want to never steal, Mr. Sheriff. No sir. I don't want God mad at me none, I don't."

"I think I believe you, young man. I believe I do. Your word is good fer me. But, I'll tell you what. I ain't going to fine you, but you've got to come in here and sweep my floor and dust everything up fer five Sattydays fer trespassin', you hear?"

"Yes sir, Mr. Sheriff. I'll be here sure enuf. You can count on me, Mr. Sheriff."

"I appreciate you comin' in here to confess. That was the right thing to do. And you don't worry none about what you seen." He put his hand on the young man's shoulder and said, "You jest keep doin' what's right, you hear? But iffen you don't come here to sweep up, you'll be in more trouble than you care to think about."

The boy stood up and shook the sheriff's hand. "Thank you, Mr. Sheriff, I'll be here tomorrow, sure. And don't you worry none. I'll be back all them Sattydays."

4 A CONFRONTATION

SOMEWHERE ALONG the line Grand became Sheriff Potter. No one knows how or why. It just happened. That's why I named these stories Potter's Tales.

A few days later Grand walked into the newspaper office and plunked down on a chair. He just sat there.

"Well, Sheriff Kranz, to what do I owe the honor of you coming in to see me?"

"Ah, Mr. Shiff, I'll let you decide the honor. Let me get to the point. I have it on the word of a reliable witness that you was in my office last May the twenty-second and about eleven o'clock in the mornin'. You riffled through my desk and found something. Then you sez, 'Ah, here it is. I knew I'd find it.' Then you snuck out the back door the same way you come in.

"Now, it 'pears to me what you was lookin' fer got back in my desk. But, I can tell it ain't the way it were. 'Sides it's got some fingerprints on it in black ink. Then you went and printed my story without my permission, but you tried to make it look like I give it to you free and willin'.

"I'll tell you what's goin' to happen. The next issue of yer paper is goin' to have an apology on the front page. You're going to name yerself for a sneak, a cheat, and a thief. You're also goin' to tell your readers that you're goin' to donate a hundred dollars fer yer wrong-doin' to the local school for some books they need. There will be no mention of this visit." With that Grand got up and walked out.

The copy boy was in the back and heard it all but he acted as if he was in the outhouse when the sheriff was up front.

That's the way Grand was. If he was angry at you and you were guilty, you'd best mind every step you took. He was the law around these parts and everybody knew it. But he could be as kind about it just as well.

5 NORALD GATSMAN

IT SEEMS THE first case Grand had when he became sheriff was about Norry Gatsmann. Norry's Pa was Henny Gatsmann. Henny's wife, Grtechen, died about a year and a half after giving birth to Norman, or Norry, as he was called. Norry never knew her, of course. Gretchen kept Henny in line while she was alive, but after her death Henny took up drinking full time. A local woman took Norry in and raised him till he was six or seven.

Then Henny wanted his son back, supposedly to help him around the place. But Norry raised himself for the most part. Norry's plight was known locally so women often brought Norry food when his father was out on a drinking spree.

As Norry grew older he learned to cook for himself but he didn't have money to buy food. He began stealing. The grocery store put up with most of it because they knew Norry's situation. A few families with money paid the bill.

But then Norry began stealing chickens from Ma Dory's hen house. Of course, Sheriff Potter knew all about Norry's exploits. The question was what to do, as something had to be done. Norry was not a bad person, just a desperate one.

Sheriff paid a visit at Henny's place. According to Grand's notes the following conversation can be constructed.

"You come here about them chickens, ain't ya? And the store, I reckon."

"I reckon so, Norry."

"Well, my paw's gone an' ain't been heard of in more'n a month and I gotta eat somehow an' I ain't got any money. So I 'spose ya kin jest stick me in jail, then you gotta feed me."

"Nope, Norry. Ain't nobody gonna go to jail and ain't nobody gonna keep on goin' hungry, neither."

"Then whut ya fixin' t'do, shoot me?"

"Now, Norry, that never come to my mind. Besides, I ain't got a gun on me to do it with. Even did I have, I'd never shoot ya. That'd be a crime even for a sheriff. Nope, yer not gonna get shot. But I do have some ideas about you living better."

After a pause, "Well, I ain't heard no ideas yet."

"Been wonderin' did ya want to hear 'em?"

"I reckon. If I got some say so about 'em."

"Ain't never gonna take yer say so away from ya. See, I've been talkin' to some folks about my ideas and with their say so I want to give you some say so. First, Ma Dory. She's gettin' older and needs help around the place. Cleanin' her chicken coop, weedin' in her garden, cleanin' up around the place and such. In return, she'll feed ya, do yer washin' and mendin'.

"Then there's Barney Slade, at the mercantile store. He needs help, too. He'll tell you about it. You kin earn some new duds yer needin'. Do a good job an' he'll give ya some cash besides.

"Then, there's George Perkins at the livery stable. He'll give ya cash fer any work ya do fer him, or you kin work to buy a horse he's got he'll sell ya. He'll hang onto the horse till you can pay it off. You'll be able to take it for rides 'n such but it'll be kept in his stable. I see you got a right good saddle hangin' there on the wall. I don't reckon yer bad at heart. Ya just need to live somehow. Now, all you have to do is give up yer sneak-thief ways and live honest. Yer say so."

"I ain't got but one problem. What if m'paw comes back. He'll figger all my stuff is hizzen 'n then he'll go 'n drink it up. 'Sides he'll whack away on me figgerin' I'm hidin' sumpthin'."

"Well, Norry. I got sumpthin' to say, but it ain't purty. Yer paw got hisself shot to death down in the saloon in Shortsville. Been wantin' to tell ya but didn't know how. Sorry I have to tell ya now, I am."

"Sheriff, I don't feel nuthin' but relief. He weren't no good to nobody, least of all me. Yer ideas are good enuf to me, but how am I goin' t'show my face at Ma Dory and that store?"

"Norry, they know your situation. They ain't mad at ya. A big apology will go a long way. That and you keepin' up yer end of the bargain."

According to Grand's notes, Norry won everybody's hearts. He never touched liquor his whole life and later bought the store when Barney decided to retire and served as the first mayor of the town.

6 THE TRACKER

AND THERE'S Grand's tracking ability.

Grand was a tracker of trackers. He learned it from an Apache Indian by the name of Red Hawk who was hailed as the best one of all time. Besides being a top-notch tracker, Grand had exceptional instincts.

A Dutchman by the name of Dick (Hendrik) Schutts moved into town. Dick was short, about five foot nine, but he was one wiry hombre with a grip of steel. And he was quick. He could move his hands faster than your eye could follow. In no time Grand had Dick as his deputy. They were always together.

Dick was light in the saddle and had a horse that was as quick on the foot as Dick was with his hands.

Dick was a fast draw, to boot. He and Grand had shoot outs just to keep in practice. Grand usually won but no one else besides Grand could out-draw Dick. He owned a brand-new Colt Dragoon revolver that he could shoot with deadly accuracy. One time he and Grand were tracking an outlaw by the name of Butch Patterson. He was a thief and a killer. He thought he was smarter than any law officer. Especially he could outwit Sheriff Potter.

One day at high noon he rode into town and robbed the mercantile store. Norry was in back putting stock on his trolley and heard the commotion. He crawled on hands and knees to peek around the corner. He got a good view of everything, even the horse out front. He hurried out of the store when Butch rode off to see which way he rode out of town.

That night he relayed it all to Sheriff Potter.

Grand and Dick tracked Butch for three days. They cornered him in his hideout. It was a rocky place so Butch could use the rocks as his cover.

Grand and Dick devised a plan. They tied up their horses on some scrub. Butch was behind the rocks. He would not be able to leave without being seen. Grand and Dick went on foot, crouching as they went along. Their idea was to draw Butch out.

At one point Dick propped his hat on a stick where he knew Butch could see just the top of it. He then climbed the rocks where he knew he could see Butch if he stood up. Grand went on ahead around the rocks. He put his hat on a stick, too, but kept walking with it in his hand. He lifted it as though he was going to stand up.

Butch saw it, stood to take a shot. Dick fired as Butch stood. His shot hit the side of Butch's gun as intended. Butch howled in pain as reverberations shot up his hands and arms and dropped the gun. Grand sprang in and in no time overpowered Butch.

Butch had evaded the law so long he became arrogant. That was part of his problem. He didn't really know Sheriff Potter when he robbed the mercantile or he would have avoided Oneida. Within twenty-four hours Butch was on his way to Lubbock, the sight of one of his most gruesome killings. He was later hanged for his crime.

Barney got all his money back and gave Norry a good reward.

Then there was that gang of rustlers. Herdsmen were losing cattle right, left, and center. They came to Grand for help. Grand formed them into a posse. They were more than eager to be part of it. Grand had a rule that he laid down. They needed to take their guns, but if anyone shot one of the rustlers, Grand would shoot him and ask questions later. They knew he meant every word he said. They agreed on the terms.

They took him to the site of the latest rustling.

"They went off this way," said the owner of the ranch.

Grand asked, "How many did they take?"

"Maybe fifteen, twenty head."

Grand looked at the ground. He followed the tracks for a ways and then came back. "They think we're stupid. They went this way." He pointed southeast. The owner looked at him and was about ready to speak. "Don't argue with me. I don't need nobody to tell me where the sun rises," Grand said through clenched teeth. "Just follow me."

(Grand would not allow anyone to distract him.)

He rode his horse at a trot for about a quarter of a mile south.

A clear trail appeared. Horse tracks, cow tracks, cow dung, and urine patches were plain in sight. The trail was going southwest.

"They got a two-day start, but they're goin' slow for the calves' sake. We'll meet them tomorrow about noon," Grand declared. "Here's our plan. Dick, I want you to pick two men and go to their stockade. It'll be in a coulee to the southeast over there. You'll find it. You know what to do. Get a couple hours rest if you need to but it'll take some good hard ridin' to get there afore their scouts report back their progress.

"The rest of us is headin' southwest. They'll be turnin' sou'east some time tomorrow. They'll have to drive their herd down between those hills yonder where they corralled the rest of yer stock. We're going to set up an ambush on either side in them hills. Give 'em a chance to surrender or get killed."

A rancher asked, "How d'ya know all this, Sheriff?"

"Been scoutin'."

"When was y'all goin' t'tell us?"

"Waitin' fer y'all t'ask fer hep."

"Well, I'll be ... What iffen we never askt?"

"Yer business."

"I'll be a broke wing crow, Sheriff, if you ain't the limit!"

"Now I want you men to listen up good. We'll wait until near sunrise before we attack. That'll give Dick time enough t'do his part."

He told then how he wanted them to position themselves and when to fire warning shots and when to shoot to kill. "Y'all just rest 'til ya hear them shots."

Everything came off as planned.

When Sheriff knew his men were in position, he called out, "Billy Joe Benjamin, you hearin' me?"

"Yeah, and who might you be?"

"Sheriff Potter. 'N I want you to call yer men by you and lay down yer weapons."

"Yer makin' me laugh, Sheriff. Y'xpect me t'come crawlin' t'you on hands and knees just for yer say so? What's one man agin' five?"

"Got a couple o'men with me."

"Ho, ho. Merry Christmas."

"Well now, din't know it were Christmas or I'da brung some presents and stuff. So yer outta luck there."

"Aint you a spoil sport," was the response.

"OK, Billy Joe, I'm finished with this. Y'all come out peaceful like or y'll get blasted out."

Sheriff heard a sharp whistle. "Tain't no use, Billy Joe, them horses are all muzzled and tied up."

Billy Joe shouted curses at his men for not shooting.

"Tain't no use, Billy Joe, them men are all muzzled and tied up, too. 'N, by the way, don't try fer yer guns 'cause we got those, too." With that he signaled to his men who were ready to act.

They cut the tie downs of the tent and pounced on Billy Joe and his moll. Billy Joe was as naked as jaybird and his moll wasn't much better. Bill's second, Grandy Pierce, and his moll were not much better off.

They soon were tied up and marched down the trail to where their horses were tied. Billy was mounted on his horse backward and his ankles tied to his stirrups. All his men on guard duty were there and tied up as well. When they were all mounted on their horses, the troop set off to the local sheriff.

They hanged rustlers in those days.

7 JACKIE BELGAR

THERE'S ANOTHER story that Grand doesn't like to talk about. I found it in his files. Again, I'm imagining the conversation that follows from the notes in the file.

The town drunk named Jackie Belgar was a braggart. Even drunk he was a fast draw. One Saturday Grand, as usual, went to the local bar. Grand didn't drink, but he liked to chat with the locals. He heard a lot, too.

Jackie came up to Grand, reached up, and flipped Grand's badge. "Hey, big shot. How's things with yer Highness? Yer nuthin' but a stuffed shirt, ya know?"

"Now, Jackie, you'd best keep your hands to yersef."

"Ho, ho, Sheriff. Din't like that, eh? Well, how 'bout this, ya like that?" That quick Jackie had his gun poking into Grand's ribs.

Grand was cool under stress. He said to Jackie, "Now, Jackie, if you pull that there trigger yer goin' to be dead yersef the next second."

Dick Shutts was there and put his gun in Jackie's back. Jackie hesitated for just a second. It gave Grand time enough to grab Jackie's hand and twist the gun away. Jackie wasn't done. He grabbed his knife and lunged for Grand. Grand deflected the knife with his left hand and punched Jackie with his right.

Grand's notes say he intended to push Jackie in his chest backward, but somehow he punched Jackie in the throat. Jackie tried to get his breath, but his throat was crushed by the punch. Grand tried to revive Jackie, but in minutes he died where he lay on the floor.

Grand said to Dick, "Go to work."

Dick immediately locked the door and began to talk to the men in the bar. There were eight men there, besides Dick and Grand. Three men said they'd seen nothing. They were facing the bar. The rest all said Jackie caused the whole ruckus. But two of them said Grand's punch was meant for Jackie's throat. However, three said Jackie was hopelessly drunk and swayed just as Grand threw his punch. Annie Catherine said, truthfully, she was filling a beer mug at the time and saw nothing.

Grand immediately stepped aside and put Dick in charge. Then Grand wrote up the incident and reported it to the state authorities. An inquest was held. Each person present, including Annie Catherine, gave a statement.

Grand was exonerated, of course, but the incident affected him deeply. He hated to kill people, no matter how guilty they were.

8 TRACKING A MURDERER

CLIVE TUSSLE was a murderer. He had no respect for human or animal life. If any man can be said to be evil to the core, it could be said of Clive. He was just as crafty as he was evil.

Clive trained himself in law and became a self-proclaimed lawyer. That was what he used to defend himself. Everyone knew he was guilty of brawls, fights, and murders. There was a string of them across central Texas. But he got off each time he defended himself in court.

He thought he was invincible. He became careless. Very few people used him as a lawyer. No one trusted him. He hired out to a cattle rancher to earn some money. The rancher, Henry Knoble, had two other hands working for him, Benny Shields and Jeff Morgan. The new man had to do the grunt work, cleaning out the horse stalls, pitching hay, hauling in grain for the horses, and currying the horses. The other hands were out on the range tending the cattle. It was a large herd, 450 head.

The calving cows needed attention. They were isolated soon after giving birth, so their calves could thrive a few weeks before being put out on the range. Clive was green with envy for these men. He thought his station in life merited a range job, but Henry didn't see it that way. Clive started to pick fights with Benny and Jeff. He picked on Jeff especially, because Jeff was not a big man. He was wiry and tough. He could stand his ground against many bigger men.

One evening Jeff was alone in the barn feeding some dogies. Clive came in and began harassing Jeff. Jeff tried to ignore Clive, which made Clive furious. He attacked Jeff. As the fight progressed, it was plain that Jeff was the stronger. Somehow Clive was able to unsheathe Jeff's knife. He killed Jeff. To make it look like self-defense, Clive cut his arm, tore his shirt and scratched himself. He made some big cuts in the legs of his jeans, scratching himself as he did so.

Unknown to Clive, Benny came in and saw all of it. Clive didn't see Benny and began to yell for help. Benny rushed up. He immediately went to the phone and called Henry in.

When Henry came in, he tried to assess the situation. Clive tried to seem upset. Benny knew Clive's reputation, so he remained quiet for the time being. Henry called for Sheriff Lorry McManus. Clive started to tell his story. Benny interrupted. He said he saw the whole thing. Clive just didn't know he did.

Clive immediately drew his pistol. Waving it back and forth, he shouted if anyone tried to stop him he'd shoot to kill. He jumped on his horse that was just outside the barn and fled.

Sheriff McManus tried to bring him down but missed his shots. He tried to find Clive's trail for weeks but found nothing. Then he heard of Grand's tracking prowess. He called on Grand, who agreed to lend a hand in trying to track and apprehend Clive Tussle.

Grand called in his sidekick Dick Shutts. The three men guessed where Clive might go and also discussed their strategy. From information they gathered, Clive headed out south-east. Grand thought it was a diversion. He was sure Clive was aiming for Mexico. Grand's theory proved to be true after their first day on the trail. Clive turned south-west.

They found his trail in Amarillo. He lingered around for two days. Grand knew Clive thought he could not be traced this far. They hit the trail to Clovis, New Mexico, and learned he'd been in the bar there two days ago. They were closing in. Clive bummed around Roswell area, chatting with people there. They caught him in a bar in Las Cruses. He was too drunk to walk straight.

Grand walked up to him and said, "Hello, Clive, let me stand you for a drink, okay?"

Clive slurred, "Tha's vera genrous of you my frien." He then looked at Grand. His face fell right off, according to Grand.

Grand ushered him out to Lorry and Dick who were waiting with the extra horse. Clive was hauled into the saddle and roped into place to prevent his falling off. When they got back, Clive was hanged on the gallows when the Judge handed down the sentence.

This is just a small part of Potter Tales, but it gives an idea of the kind of sheriff Gresham Potter Kranz III turned out to be.

ADVENTURES OF A SQUIRREL NAMED SQUIGGLES

I'd like to tell you the story of a squirrel named Squiggles. I first saw Squiggles in my backyard after my granddaughter came running into the house chattering about a funny squirrel that, in her words, "always jumped all around and never stood still for even a little minute. You should see him, Grandpa," she said, all excited. So I went out to see him. This is his story.

1 SQUIGGLES IS BORN

SQUIGGLES WAS BORN in a nest, which his mother had built, high up in an old oak tree in our back yard. It was in a warm and comfy nest; at least a squirrel would think so. I suppose you wouldn't, unless you would like to live in a cramped little space made of twigs and leaves and little bits of this and that. Remember that your house is high up in a tree. It would sway back and forth when the wind blew and dust would get in your eyes. You might even get an upset tummy or a little scared, but not squirrels. They like it that way or else they wouldn't build those nests high in the trees.

Well, anyway, when Squiggles was born up in that nest in the old oak tree, his two brothers and sister were born at the same time. Mother Squirrel thought that this was an average, ordinary, everyday, not unusual little squirrel family. But, oh boy, was she in for a big surprise!

One of her babies was anything but an average, ordinary, everyday, not unusual little squirrel. Squiggles was different from his two brothers and sister. Oh yes, he was very different; different from the tip of his nose to the last hair on the end of his tail. You see, from the tip of that nose to the end of that tail, Squiggles was a squiggler. And a squiggler is not average, not ordinary, not usual, not an everyday squirrel in any way. Yes, a squiggler is unusual!

Now you may ask what is a squiggler? I'll tell you. But it may take this whole story to really tell you what a squiggler is. In short, it is much more than a wriggler and it is definitely more than a squirmer! Squiggles wriggled and squirmed and squirmed and wriggled all at the same time. That little squirrel was never quiet for two eye-blinks in a row.

Squiggles squiggled this way. He squiggled that way. He squiggled up. He squiggled down. He squiggled all around. And all the time his little tail was curled up over his back and twitching the way the rest of Squiggles did.

Mother Squirrel never knew if the nest was shaking from the wind or from her squiggler. Sometimes she really needed to get some rest. So she would curl up in a little ball and put Squiggles right between her front paws. She would hold him very close and wrap her big bushy tail around her little squiggler.

Squiggles would hear his mother's heartbeat go thumpity, thumpity, thumpity, thumpity, thumpity. And because his little tummy was full from eating at his mother's milk station, he would get sleepy, sooo sleepy that he would make a great big yawn. And then he would almost stop squiggling.

Then he would take another bigger, great big yawn. Then he would finally stop squiggling and fall fast asleep. Then all the squirrels in that nest would finally get some rest. But it wouldn't be long and Squiggles would wake up again. And then it was squiggle, squiggle, squiggle, squiggle some more. And everybody wished that Squiggles would sleep a little longer. Maybe two or three days.

2 SQUIGGLES GROWS BIGGER

NOW SQUIGGLES' little sister was named Fluff. His little brothers were named Guff and Stuff. Well, Fluff and Guff and Stuff could not stand Squiggles squiggling all the time. They would complain to their mother that this nest was too little for them if Squiggles was going to squiggle all the time.

But Mother Squirrel didn't know what to do. So she just told them that soon they would all grow big enough that they could leave the nest. Then life in that old oak tree would be better.

She told them that because she was sure that Squiggles was going to be out first because he was growing so big so fast. And she was right. It wasn't long and Squiggles found his way out onto the branches around the nest. Fluff and Guff and Stuff were really glad for that. When Squiggles was gone they would curl up and take a good long nap.

The first time he was out, Squiggles scared himself half to death. He lost his footing and nearly fell off the branch! He was hanging on by only one paw. He looked down. It looked like an awful long way to the ground, so he worked hard, very hard. He swung his tail and his back paws and finally he was able grab the branch with two paws, then three, and finally he got all four paws on the branch and was able to climb back to safety.

Then he scurried back into his mother's nest. His little heart wasn't going thumpity, like his mother's. It was too little yet, so it was going thimpity, thimpity, thimpity, thimpity, thimpity and ten times as fast as his mother's. Well, almost ten times as fast.

But once Squiggles had been out of that nest, it was just too small for him anymore. As soon as his little heart started doing thimpity, thimpity, thimpity, a little slower, he was back out onto that branch again. He soon was running up and down the branch as if he had been doing it from the day he was born. Sometimes he would slide a little way off the branch. He discovered that it was a super good thing that his mother gave him a tail. His tail was perfect for helping him to balance himself.

He also discovered that he had some good claws at the end of his paws. They came in handy, because one time he did fall. He became careless and fell right off the branch. Down he went. Squiggles had never been so scared in his little life!

But he stuck out his paws with the claws and grabbed for the branch that was hurrying past him. By now those claws on his paws were working very well indeed. They stuck onto the branch and Squiggles came to a dead stop so fast he thought he was going to lose he paws with the claws, but they stayed with him.

Quickly he crawled back up onto that branch. He looked up. His nest seemed far away now. But he didn't even think of running back to his mother. He had something else in mind.

He ran down the branch to the trunk of the tree. He climbed back up the trunk to his home branch. That was fun, he thought. So this time he did it all over again. Only this time he did it on purpose. He kept climbing up and falling off that branch and catching himself until he was tired.

3 SQUIGGLES AND THE STORM

EVERY DAY, bright and early, Squiggles was out of the nest. He would play on the branches and up and down the tree. He would chase Fluff and Guff and Stuff and they would chase him until they all got tired out. Then he would eat soft little branches and buds that grew on the tree they lived in.

Later his mother taught him and his sister and brothers to hunt for their own food on the ground. He learned to smell where acorns were buried. He dug them up and ate them. They were so good he would hunt until his tummy was so full he could hardly run up the tree. He would lie on a branch to sun himself until he was ready to play again.

One day the sun didn't come out the whole day. Squiggles wondered why. That night he found out. He went to sleep early because it was so dark. All of a sudden something bounced him wide-awake. He didn't know what it was.

The whole world lit up. He thought maybe the sun came out after all. But the light lasted a very short time. Then a big loud boom nearly broke his eardrums.

Squiggles had never heard such a noise. Every hair on his little body stood straight out. His tail was as big and round as a great big bottlebrush. He shook and shivered with fear and he wasn't squiggling a bit. He was shaking all over from the scare of that big boom.

The wind began to blow. His nest went up and down farther and faster than he thought it could. It swayed from side to side until even his tummy began to feel a little sick. To top it all off, it began to rain great big drops. Squiggles had never seen or felt rain. Some of it came into the nest. He didn't like it at all.

He wanted the wind to stop. He wanted the rain to stop. But it didn't stop at all for a long time. Just when Squiggles thought the nest was going to fall, the wind died down, but the rain kept up all night. In the morning it finally quit.

He went out with the rest of his family to look around. He was almost too shaky to hunt for his breakfast. That was one night that Squiggles didn't squiggle very much. He hoped it would never storm like that again.

Squiggles noticed that the branch was wet. His little paws and legs got wet. First he would shake this paw. Then he would shake that one. Then he would shake the other one and then the last one.

The fur on his tummy got wet so he shook himself all over. He didn't like all the wet stuff. He did discover, though, that it tasted good. He licked some of the wet off his front paw. It was good. He licked some off the branch. That was even better.

He ran down the tree. It was wet all the way down. When he was on the grass he found out that the grass was wet but the water on the grass tasted best of all.

The air was so fresh and clean that it made him want to jump. So he jumped. When he landed the water on the grass splashed everywhere. He got wet all over, even in his eyes and ears. Yuck! That didn't feel good at all, so he climbed the tree and shook himself off again.

Squiggles decided that breakfast would be some of the acorns off the tree this morning. It was just too wet in the grass to hunt for buried acorns, but he liked the buried ones better.

4 SQUIGGLES GETS A BATH

ONE DAY Squiggles was hunting for some acorns. His mother and Fluff and Guff and Stuff were doing the same thing.

Squiggles sat up. He saw something he had not seen before. It had a big leg, but only one leg. He took a few hops closer. It had a big round flat thing on the top of the leg. It looked just about high enough for him to jump up on it so he could see what it was.

Squiggles' mother saw him looking at the thing. She barked at him, warning him not to try to jump up on it. Squiggles didn't see any reason why not. So he took a little run and jumped. He missed and landed flat on his tummy on the ground. Plop! That didn't feel so good. He stood up, shook himself to make sure he was all right, and decided to jump again.

His mother barked at him a little louder this time. Squiggles wasn't listening. He ran and jumped again. This time he just got his claws on the edge, but the whole thing moved just enough to make him fall off. Now he was determined to try again. His mother didn't bark this time. She just sat up and watched.

Squiggles took a little longer run and jumped a little higher. He grabbed the edge of the thing but all of a sudden he felt himself falling. The whole thing tipped over. Squiggles fell on his back. The thing fell right in front of him and a whole ocean of water flooded over Squiggles. It gave Squiggles a bath like he had never had before. He was wet in front. He was wet in back. He was wet on top. He was wet under his tummy. He was wet on his head. He was wet on his tail and all the way in between his head and tail.

Squiggles got up and shook himself. Little drops of water flew everywhere. He did not like feeling wet and his tail hurt where that awful thing fell on top of it. He was angry at that thing for falling on him. He barked at it like his mother barked at him. But the worst part was that all the squirrels around laughed at him.

"Next time I'll do it so it won't land on me," he said to himself as he ran around the thing to see what it was.

His mother said, "That's a bird bath, silly. It wasn't meant for squirrels." She ran up the tree to her nest.

Just then Squiggles heard a loud bang. It scared him. He sat up on his hind legs and looked. He saw a great big thing coming out of the strangest tree he had ever seen. It was the oddest squirrel he had ever seen. It was coming toward him. Quick as a wink he dashed up his mother's tree.

"Mother, mother," he panted, half out of breath. "I just saw a great big squirrel. It was almost as big as the tree. It came out of a big tree thing and was walking on its back legs and had some funny fur all over it and, and. . ."

"That was not a squirrel, my child," interrupted his mother. "That is a people. You are scared and well you should be. Don't ever go near a people. They are dangerous. Do you hear me? And that big thing is their nest. They call it a house."

Squiggles felt a little shy. He said very meekly, "Yes, Mama." But he added, "Why do people squirrels live in those big things?"

"Never you mind about that. You just stay far away and don't get hurt," Mama said.

5 SQUIGGLES FORGETS

THE NEXT DAY Squiggles forgot all about his mama's warning. When he ran down the tree to go look for his breakfast, the people squirrel came out of the thing again. Squiggles was scared. He wiggled and squirmed. He jumped all about. He chased his tail and rolled over. But for some reason he couldn't run away.

After a while he stopped being so afraid. Then he found out why he couldn't run away. His nose was telling him not to. He smelled something very good. It made him jump and squirm and wiggle all over again.

It made the little girl laugh. Only Squiggles did not know it was a little girl and he did not know that she was laughing. To a squirrel she was just making funny noises.

Just then another people squirrel came out of the thing – uh, box – uh, house. That made Squiggles run up the tree. It was just too scary. He ran to his mother.

What he didn't know was this. It was the little girl's mother who came out of the house. The girl said to her mother, "Did you see that little squirrel? That's the little squirrel. He jumps all over. He turns around and chases his tail. He doesn't stand still for a minute. He's funny. He squirms and he wiggles all over all the time. I'm going to name him Squiggles."

And that's how Squiggles got his name. But Squiggles didn't hear it; he was up in the tree with his mother.

"Mother! Mother! A bigger people squirrel just came out of the thing."

"That big people is the mother of the other one," she said. "It's just like us. Go play, but do be careful and don't get into trouble."

Squiggles felt jumpy all over. But he ran down the tree. The big people squirrel was gone. Just the little one was there. He smelled the good smell again. O, how he wanted what she had.

Then he saw her bend down. She put her front paw (Squiggles didn't know it was a hand, you see) on the ground and then stood up and backed away.

Squiggles sat up on his back legs for a long time just looking but the little people squirrel did not move. Squiggles didn't either. Then he went down on all fours, jumped ahead a little, and sat back up to look again.

The little people squirrel was still there. That good smell was even stronger now. Two more hops. Almost there. A big jump. Grab and run. He had the nut. He sat up to taste it. Mmm! It was good. He ate every bit of it.

From that day on, Squiggles wanted those nuts. They were much better than acorns. The little people squirrel kept bringing more and more. Sometimes his brothers and sister would get some too. But they were more afraid than Squiggles. So Squiggles got to have most of them. Eating all those nuts was making Squiggles grow fat and his fur very slick and shiny.

He was also growing less and less afraid of the little people squirrel. She talked to him a lot, but he didn't understand it. He just knew he liked all those nuts she kept giving to him. Each day he went a little closer because the little people squirrel put the nuts closer to her.

Then one day she kept it in her paw—hand, that is. Squiggles was afraid, but the smell of the nut was too strong. He took the nut and ran away. The little people squirrel jumped up making all kinds of noises and ran into the big house. He didn't know that she was laughing and telling her mother what had just happened.

Soon Squiggles was not afraid at all. He would run up the little girl's arm and sit on her shoulder. It was such fun. Mother and Fluff and Guff and Stuff thought he was crazy, but Squiggles was having too much fun to stop.

6 SQUIGGLES' FIRST WINTER

SQUIGGLES WAS nice and fat now and he wasn't squiggling so much anymore. He had an urge to build a nest. So he did. He built it in a tree near his mother's tree. It was getting cold outside and he felt like he wanted to go to sleep soon.

Then one day a lot of white stuff began falling from the sky. He ran down his tree and up the other to his mother, who told him that this was snow. He should go to his nest and sleep as long as he wanted to. So he did.

He slept a long time. Once in a while he would wake up and go looking for food. It was not easy. The ground was hard and cold. Mostly he had to eat what he could find on the trees. Sometimes he could find an acorn or two or the tender ends of branches. Then he would go back to sleep for another long time.

When it was very cold Squiggles would eat as fast has he could. Then he would hurry back to his comfy nest to sleep again. Once when he woke up he went out of his nest. His claws could hardly grip the branches. They were slick and cold. Can you guess what had happened? While Squiggles was asleep there was an ice storm. Everything was coated with ice. Squiggles just hurried back into his nest to sleep some more.

Finally winter turned to spring. Squiggles was glad. The snow was gone. It was not easy to find the acorns under the hard ground, but then a wonderful thing happened. The people squirrel came out of the box again. There were more nuts. Squiggles had a feast and grew fat again.

7 A BIG SURPRISE

SQUIGGLES SEEMED to be growing too fat. The people squirrel didn't bring so many nuts. Squiggles wondered why. His tummy wanted those nuts. The little people squirrel told him he was too fat, but Squiggles didn't understand that at all.

The other squirrels thought Squiggles was too fat, too. Mamma squirrel just smiled and went up the tree. Squiggles went to his nest and stayed there for a long time. When he came out, everybody got a big surprise. Behind Squiggles came four little baby squirrels.

How could that be? All the trees were buzzing with the news. Squiggles had some baby squirrels?

Mamma squirrel just smiled. She didn't know what all the fuss was about. She knew all along that Squiggles was not a boy squirrel, she knew Squiggles was a girl squirrel. Why did everybody think a squiggler could only be a boy squirrel? Sometimes a squiggler is a girl squirrel, just like with people. The good thing is that squigglers usually stop sguiggling when they grow up. Squiggles had stopped squiggling, too.

As for Squiggles, she just hoped none of her babies was a squiggler like she had been. And her hope came true, not one of her babies was a squiggler. And Mama Squiggles was happy. So was Gramma Squirrel.

THE STORY OF HENDRIK DeKAST

A Parable

ALMOST AS SOON as I arrived at my new pastorate I began to hear of a person by the name of Henk DeKast. After some inquiry I was told there was a relative of his living in a nearby town who would tell me the story. I phoned him and he gladly agreed to have me over and fill me in.

"Hello and welcome. So you want to know the story of Henk DeKast? When you phoned I told you to come over and I'd tell you, so come on in. I know the story quite well because I heard it many times. I am a grandson of Margareta. GranGran was still alive when I first remember hearing this story. She filled in a lot of details, even some intimate stuff that Grandma didn't know or didn't want to tell. And I won't let that out."

The following is that account arranged somewhat chronologically.

Hendrik (Henk) DeKast was the fourth of seven children born to Teunis (Teun) DeKast and his wife, Hendrika (Rika) Van Trekvoorst. Margareta was the oldest, next came Cornelius, then Jacob. Marika followed Henk; Franck followed them, and last was Elizabet.

Teun was a hard-bitten Dutchman who kept his wife and children firmly under his thumb. He tried to dictate each and every move they made, but the more he tried, the more they did everything they could to defy him behind his back.

Margareta married when she was barely eighteen. Neal and Jake left home to join the army as soon as they were old enough.

81

The war had just broken out and they saw it as a way to leave home. Neal was killed in action on D-Day on Normandy Beach. Jake was sent to the Pacific theater and sustained a severe head wound on some remote island, which left him without a memory or anything else, really. He was in a military hospital somewhere in the Pacific, but he was in no condition to be moved. He died of pneumonia a few months after he was injured. None of the family ever saw either of them alive after they went overseas.

Henk was deferred because farm work was considered an essential industry in those days, and partly because the draft board thought that two brothers killed in action was enough for one family. He was glad to stay home because he knew his mother needed that.

The death of two of his sons didn't do much to change Teun for the better. In fact, he became worse. One day, when he was especially angry and abusive, Henk could take it no longer. He walked up close to Teun, looked him in the face, and said, "If you keep this up, I'm leaving just as Neal and Jake did. I'll stay here and help but only if you stop the craziness. I'm not staying around for you, I'm doing it for Ma. But get it through your thick head I will take no more of your s—!" He stood staring straight into his father's face without flinching.

To Henk's utter surprise Teun just stood there with an open mouth. After a while Teun turned around and went back to work. Not a word was said about it openly, though it was whispered about quietly in their bedrooms.

You see, Elizabet had come into the barn to collect the eggs from the chicken's nests and heard it all. Teun and Henk had not seen her; they were in a lot behind the barn, so they each assumed the matter was just between the two of them. That incident did serve to bring a measure of peace to the household they had never known before. Henk, for himself, determined then and there he would never be like his father. He would not make life a living hell for his family.

Not long after that incident, Teun took sick. He had always been a heavy smoker. Cigars, pipes, and then tailor-mades when they came out. His lungs were filling up the doctor said and his heart was being squeezed to death by the buildup of fluid around it. Besides, as best he could tell, blood was not getting to Teun's head any more like it should. When he made a house call, he would feel Teun's neck and shake his head.

A stroke was imminent, he told Hendrika one day. Teun was barely 56 years old when the doctor's words came true. Teun went into a fit of coughing one night and died of a stroke.

The whole town and countryside came to the funeral. Teun was thought of as a good man by most people. He was a respected man in the church and community. He was always fair and honest in his business dealings. He served two terms as Deacon in his church (First Christian) and had just been elected as an Elder before he took sick and died. How was anyone to know what went on beyond the gate to that farm? Sad to say, his family didn't miss him much when he was gone.

Henk stayed on and worked the farm for a few years and did quite well. His ingenuity, which he inherited from his father, plus his father's other redeeming feature, left the family well off financially. Teun was as tight-fisted as he was hard-bitten. He sank every last penny into paying off the farm. He did not believe in debt even if it meant meager helpings of food on the table and not a very comfortable home to live in. So the family was not under a mountain of debt when Teun passed on. Added to this was the fact that farm income was on the rise in those days as was the price for land.

One afternoon Hendrika chose to bring coffee to Henk out on the back forty where he was plowing. While he ate she said to him,

"Henk, I've made up my mind about something. Now you hear me before you say anything. You're working this farm real good. You're making us do very well. But you ain't been getting paid what you're worth. I want to sell you the farm for half-price. You've earned that and more. Even at half-price it is more than we bought it for. And with the money you'll be paying me I could build a house down there near the corner for me and the younger kids. Elizabet loves the farm, too, and she could keep on taking care of the animals and such while you farm…Just a minute, I ain't finished too yet. Besides, you need to be thinking about getting married and…"

"Ma," said Henk, chewing a mouth full of roast beef sandwich, "I appreciate that, but…"

"Now, you listen here, Hendrik Pieter DeKast" (Henk knew when she added his middle name he'd best shut up and listen) "I've made up my mind and that's all there is going to be to it! I had Marga take me to the bank the other day and it's all settled. All you have to do is go in and sign some papers. I knew you would try to talk me out of it, but now it's done. And done is done!"

They sat in total silence for a while, Hendrika on the tongue of the plow and Henk with his back against a tractor wheel. Finally Henk said,

"OK, Ma. I guess that's the way you want it. I want you to know how much I appreciate it. I would have kept it the way it was, for my part. I don't want you and the kids to ever be without on my account. I've got some savings, too."

Hendrika stood up and so did Henk. She took his hand. With tears in her eyes she said, "Henk, you keep your savings for yourself. You've been a good son. You mean more to me than you'll ever know."

She kissed him on the cheek and quickly turned to go back to the house.

And so it was. When Hendrika's house was ready, Henk with her agreement tore down the old house (not much more than a shack) and had a nice one built in its place. Now he was ready to look for a wife. He knew just where he would start.

Jan Fedder had a daughter about Henk's age, Dorothy. She had gotten married to Ben Bruinekool just before he was drafted. He was killed in the Battle of the Bulge and she had never remarried, though a few eligible men had courted her.

She was pretty, but shy. She had stayed at home with her folks when Ben went overseas and stayed on after his funeral. Jan and Griet had only the one child, so they were glad to have her in the house.

She had a desk job at the lumberyard of the local Farmer's Co-op. Henk often came to the lumberyard and secretly Dottie thought that big red-headed Dutchman was a handsome fellow, but that's as far as it went. The guys at the yard often kidded her about him, but she just laughed it off.

She knew him well enough. He often came to their place to talk things over with her father and sometimes stayed for supper, but that was just a custom among the farmers. Besides, she was sure she would never marry again. And, if she had thought about it at all, she would have told herself Henk was not the marrying kind.

So when Henk started coming over to their place a little oftener, she didn't take any notice. But then, one Sunday night after church, Henk asked if he could take her home. She agreed, but didn't know why, except she knew her ma had invited Hendrika over that night for a visit, so why not?

When she made to get out of the car and go into the house, Henk stopped her.

"I have something I'd like to say, Dottie. I don't know no other way than to say it straight like I'm thinking it. I have the house and the farm I'm on and I need someone to take care of the house and yard and such and if you'd...I mean I'm asking you to marry me and be my wife.

"I know this has to be a shock to you, but hear me out. I wouldn't expect anything from you. I mean, I know you loved another man and probably still do, and that's OK with me. We could work things out. There's plenty of room in the house, if you know what I mean.

"Well, I've said enough. Thursday night is Ascension Day service and I'll take you home after and you can give me your answer. If you say no, nothing more will ever be said by me about it again. OK?"

Dottie sat there as shocked as she could be, and totally speechless. As she got out of the car, Henk did too and walked her to the house.

On Tuesday after work she went to Henk's place. She found him in the barn. He looked up, surprised.

Dottie said to him, "I couldn't wait till Thursday. I've made up my mind. I'm accepting your proposal. I'll be your wife."

Now it was Henk's turn to be shocked. He thought he had blown it completely and was sure she was going to turn him down and probably never speak to him again. He had tears in his eyes and could hardly talk. When he got his voice back they talked for a while. Then Dottie went home.

Henk told his mother that night and Dottie told her folks. When they all got over their shock, they all agreed it was a good idea, but a bit of a strange way of going about things. But then, Henk didn't always do things the usual way.

That Saturday they went to get a marriage license and the following Saturday the parents gathered in the preacher's house as witnesses as Hendrik Pieter DeKast and Dorothy Frieda Bruinekool were married.

One evening a few months later, Henk was sitting in his big easy chair with his feet up on a hassock reading a farm magazine. After a while he became aware that something was different in the room, but couldn't place it. All of a sudden it came to him. Dottie and Ben's wedding picture wasn't on the bureau anymore. He had told her she could keep it there, he didn't mind. But now he wondered what to do.

Then he thought of something.

He got up and said, "I'd like a cup of hot tea. I'll make one for you too if you like."

Dottie said that would be nice and wondered what was going on. Henk came back in a short while with the full teacups with a cookie tucked next to the cup on each saucer. He set them on the table next to Dottie. Then he put one hand on her shoulder and lifted her chin with the other and planted a huge kiss on Dottie's lips and said:

"I love you Dorothy Frieda DeKast."

Dottie was so shocked by Henk's actions her arms dropped to the side of the chair and she nearly slid right off it. The sock she was mending with the darning egg in the toe hit the floor with a clatter and went skittering off with the sock top flapping along behind it. Henk had to literally hold her up from falling. When she recovered a bit she said,

"You might give a person a little warning what you're up to, you know."

Then she got up, took Henk by the hand, and led him to her bedroom.

"This is where you belong from now on, Henk Pieter DeKast. I love you too, you big handsome Dutchman!"

Dottie nearly laughed out loud to see the tea and cookies still on the table the next morning. Hmm! Cold tea and a slightly stale and chewy cookie tasted pretty good as a celebration, she discovered.

Nine months later, Hendrik Pieter DeKast Jr. was born. Now there are proud papas, but none was so proud as Henk DeKast Sr. the day young Henk was baptized. His presence practically filled the whole church all by itself. And nobody begrudged him a bit.

In time they had a little girl and another boy. And the DeKast family prospered. Henk was always reading farm magazines and was quick to see how he could improve his yields and his income. When combines first came out, Henk bought one.

The farmers in the church did all they could to keep from laughing in Henk's face. They were sure Henk was going to harvest a small crop with that thing and lose his shirt this time. It was sure to waste oats galore, they thought. They would kid him about his eighteen-bushel and acre oats, but Henk would just smile and walk away.

A couple of the men asked him seriously what his yield was. He said it was about three bushel an acre more than he had ever gotten; he was getting close to twenty-five bushels. He pointed out the grain was handled only once instead of four times the old way. And that meant a lot less grain falling to the ground. Farmers began hiring him and his machine to bring in their grain. Henk soon paid off his new machine. But you never saw Henk gloating or laughing at the nay-sayers.

When contour farming came along, Henk was again one of the first to see its value. It kept the rain from running off the land and since the tractor was always working on the level, he saved a lot on gas. So, Henk and Dottie DeKast prospered.

As they prospered Henk became more generous. A young man from a poor family in the church decided he wanted to become a minister. He was prepared for a difficult time paying his way; his family couldn't help him much. But at registration at the denominational college he found his tuition was already paid. That went on through his four college and three seminary years. Those who knew this suspected who was the generous donor, but no one said it out loud. They just thanked God in their hearts for a man like Henk DeKast.

Henk had served as Deacon and was in his third term as an Elder when perhaps the most important of all incidents took place. Henk Jr. was in post-grad work at an Agricultural University, Beatrice was in nursing school, and Daniel was in college, too.

One Sunday on the way to church, Henk stopped the car and told Dottie to go on to church, but don't ask any questions.

She trusted her husband implicitly and went on to church.

After the service one of the Elders asked Dottie where Henk was. Before she could reply, a voice popped up and said, loud enough for all around to hear,

"Ya vant to know vere Henk DeKast iss? I tell ya vere he iss. He's mit his hired hand out by Cliff Miller pootin' op hay bayles, dats vere he iss. En ya asks me, it's a cryin' shame, too yet, dat an Elder vat is vice-presidents of de Gunsistory is makin' hay op Sondag. I saw him mit mine own two eyes, so don' say I'm going to make up ein storie yust for fun, too."

Dottie was not surprised by what Sjoerd Schimpen said. She knew where Henk was. She just did not like the way Sjoerd made his speech so public. But within thirty seconds it was all around the church and in another ninety it had gone at least five miles into the countryside.

Voices of all kinds were heard.

"Well, I'm not that surprised. Henk never did seem that sincere to me, if I may say so."

"I never thought a man would stoop that low. It's a positive shame."

"Well, he sure knew how to make our church a laughing-stock, that's for sure."

"Yeh. How'll we ever be able to tell our kids to keep the Sabbath day holy now?"

"Yep, he ruined that, alright."

"I wonder what the preacher is going to make of this? Him and Henk are thick as thieves. This will sure put him on the spot. We'll know what he's made of now for sure."

"Take it easy. I know Henk. He'll have a good reason for doing what he did, I'm sure. I think we should not rush to judgment and give the man a chance. It was going to rain..."

"Sure, it was going to rain. What of that? I had hay down, too, but I was in church. Sure, if it rains my hay won't be so good. Sometimes you have to leave such things in the Lord's hands."

"How could you ever defend a sin this big? No man should ever have an excuse for doing such an awful thing. Don't try to defend him."

"If Henk wanted to do something, he could give Cliff some of his own hay and take the rained on stuff. He didn't have to violate the Sabbath to help the man out."

Such voices and many more were heard for days. The telephone lines were hot with talk.

As for Dottie, she had gone to Sarah Miller to help her prepare dinner for the men that Sunday.

It rained all day Monday and drizzled Tuesday.

By Monday night Cliff had been told what was happening in the church. Early on Tuesday he went to Henk to talk to him. He found Henk in the barn cool as a cucumber, humming a tune.

"How can you be so cool at a time like this? Look what I've done to you."

"You didn't do a thing to me, Cliff. I knew you needed help and I did my best to lend a hand. You needed that hay put in your barn without rain, I know that and you do too, I think. It's been tough for you lately and with your hired hand out sick and not knowing when he'll be back. Well, you needed help. I knew there would be a ruckus, but it'll die down and no one will be the worse off for it."

"At least let me pay for your man's work."

"Nothing doing. I came of my own free will and I asked my man to come too. I paid him already and he was glad to come. If you had asked us to help, I'd let you pay him, but not now. Some day I may need your help, so we'll leave it at that."

Cliff fidgeted in silence for a while. Henk could tell he was agitated about something.

Finally Cliff said, "There's something else. You did what nobody else would do. You were willing to break an important rule of your church to help me. Why? You never work on Sunday."

"I believe one of the reasons God put us on this earth is to help each other. I know you have a struggle right now and that's no secret. Something inside me told me to help you out, Sunday or no Sunday. It just seemed more important to give you a hand."

"Henk, that's just it. That's just the way you are. You know I've always held you off when you tried to talk to me about religion and such. You never pushed me and I appreciate that. But now I'm asking you how does a person become a believer in God and a church-goer like you? You know what I mean? You've got something I need and I want to know how to get it."

Henk breathed a prayer and then began by telling him about God's grace. "We don't earn or merit standing with God, it's a gift from him. When we see our need, he's there to fill it with his goodness and love. Jesus came to earth to take on our flesh and blood to do what we can't do, save ourselves from our sin. He took our sin on himself and went to the cross with it. He was able to overcome death and the devil and set us free from all sin. Our part is now to live for him in all we do as a way to show how thankful we are for his gift."

When he finished, he asked Cliff if it was all right that they prayed together. Henk then thanked God for Cliff's interest in knowing about him and his salvation. He thanked God that he was there with his grace to give Cliff a new heart.

Before Henk was done with his prayer, Cliff was in tears and so was Henk. They sat on those hay bales a while. When he was able, Cliff told Henk what a wonderful peace was in his heart. If Henk hadn't come on Sunday, he'd probably still be his same old self.

Then he wanted to know what to do now. Henk suggested they study the Bible together. Cliff didn't have one, so Henk went into the house to get one of theirs and promised Cliff to get him a new one. He also got an old Psalter Hymnal with the Catechism in the back. He asked Cliff to read some of that and they'd get together for some study in a few days.

The next day the preacher phoned and asked if he could come over Thursday morning to talk. When he came he said he wanted to hear Henk's side of the situation. Henk told him all of it, why he did it and what had happened from it. The preacher was silent. Then Henk handed him a letter. He said it was his resignation from the Consistory. Henk was sure this was the best way to go. He was sure no one would in good conscience be able to take communion from him at this point.

The preacher read Henk's letter on Sunday and everyone assumed Henk had resigned because the preacher laid down the law to him. Well, well, the preacher had a good backbone after all, they thought. Henk and Dottie kept attending church but were given the cold shoulder for the most part.

However, when Henk and Dottie went to Cliff and Mary's place for the Bible study, they were surprised to see Cliff's brother Ed and his wife there and Mary's sister Flossie and her husband. By the end of the fourth week, Henk and Dottie were nurturing six new Christians. Then the subject of church attendance came up. Cliff was not ready to go to First Church. He just felt he could not face that bunch. Henk suggested they go to the Methodist Church. Cliff wanted Henk and Dottie to go along, which they did. Because of that they soon had the Methodist minister in their bible study. He wanted to know what was going on. In no time he was preaching from the Heidelberg Catechism on Sunday.

Henk and Dottie kept going to First Church on Sunday evenings. They still got the cold shoulder, though a few were warming up a little. They refrained from taking communion so as not to stir up more trouble.

Then one evening they ran flat into Sjoerd on the way out of church. Henk held out his hand. Sjoerd finally took it reluctantly. Henk invited him over to talk. He said it would do both of them good to sit down and air their differences with each other. Sjoerd mumbled a decline, but he didn't badmouth Henk much after that. In fact, he soon stopped altogether. And he started attending the Baptist church.

After things had cooled down mostly, the people of First Church began to reluctantly voice another view of things. Perhaps if they had treated Henk a little differently, maybe First Church would be growing like the Methodists were. But then the Methodists were pretty lax in who they let into the church, you know. Church purity was important, too.

The Deacons did note that the offerings for missions grew somewhat and at the annual report that gave cause for some talk and seemed to salve their collective conscience a little.

But the Methodists continued to grow. First Church even lost a few of the young people who married into the Methodists and that rankled a few pretty badly. Mixed marriages were frowned on.

On Sunday evenings, however, families would get together in each other's homes and church matters would inevitably come up. They would discuss the purity of the church, the pure preaching of the Word, the right administration of the sacraments, and proper discipline. In that light First Church definitely came out ahead, no matter what anyone said. Even the official Church Visitors praised First Church for how things were.

But the Methodist church continued to grow.

Henk continued farming well into his seventies. On retiring he sold the farm to Cliff Miller and his sons and retired into town. An old leg injury flared up later and put Henk in the hospital for a few days.

One Saturday afternoon the conversation among the men who lined the wall in the local barbershop turned to Henk and his troubles.

A man leaned forward in his chair and said to Sjoerd Schimpen, "You had a run-in with Henk, too, didn't you, Sjoerd?"

There was a sudden silence in the room, but the chairs seemed to be wiggling a lot. Sjoerd said, "Ja, dat's true. But I gotta add somting to dat story. I just come out da hospital. I visit to Henk en his wife. I told him wit shame in my face dat I didn't treat dem so good as I should. He did it right, I told him. He lived his Gristian faith in da right way. He was ready to step on my toes and lots more to do da right ting. He was ready to break a few church rules besides to help a man wat needs help. If der was more like him der would be more Cliffses in churches.

"I wants to say more but Henk just takes my hand in his big one and says, 'I want to shake hands with a Gristian brother. Sjoerd will you say a prayer for me and my wife?'

"And it just now pops in mine head dat he is still doing da same ting in dat hospital bed. He's a perty big man iss all I can say."

For while the buzz of the hair clipper and the snip of the scissors was the only sound in the room.

THE MARRIAGE

Jake and Rhonda, (not their actual names) both approved the following account of marital counselling sessions they attended.

I wanted to record it, because, in my estimation, many elements of the problems they faced are typical of other marriages. Their approval gave me the impetus necessary to write it up.

Introduction

JAKE AND RHONDA, as with many couples, approached the problems they faced from an immature perspective. They had no awareness of this, of course, but needed to learn it. They fought the way children fight. Children fight without resolution; they simply choose to put it behind them. Though adults try this, they seldom succeed.

Adults allow grudges and resentments to build up, which makes true marital intimacy impossible. Couples usually react to 'patterns of behavior' or 'what she/he means' when certain body language or words or phrases appear in their conversation. Instead of reacting to the immediate situation, the past is often used as a club.

Rhonda's desire to see Jake change is another typical stance in many marriages. It is the typical 'I'm OK, you are not OK' syndrome that destroys personal growth and marital intimacy. Most often the wife verbalizes this perspective, however, men feel it as well but prefer to 'live and let live' rather than voice it.

Rhonda's anger is atypical to a degree. However, anger on the part of one partner or the other is not unusual. As with Rhonda, it is an attempt to control. It is often effective, though destructive, in the marriage. They learn it does not control the counselor, which becomes a high hurdle for one or both parties.

Anger is also a way to avoid the real problems within the angry person.

Next, the lists of grievances a couple have toward each other are usually accurate. Such lists reflect problems that need to be addressed. The difficulty is created when either, or both, think the resolution of their problems is for the other person to change. It is difficult for one partner, or both, to be willing to be vulnerable and admit the need for personal change.

Jake's desire to prove to Rhonda he changed is less typical but often appears, most often in men. Such acceptance of blame is helpful but not a resolution. It underscores the accuracy of the partner's claims. The problem is it tends to yield control of the marriage to the other person, leaving them feeling justified in their stance of superiority. The other partner needs to be exceptionally mature to weather such a maternal stance.

Jake's rapid progress is not typical. It shows, however, what can happen when one or the other party strongly desires to change. His extraordinary intelligence was a huge asset for Jake. He was exceptional in his willingness to see the disparity between his business and personal personae. Once he grasped it, his growth was phenomenal.

Jake also demonstrated an unusual willingness to be vulnerable and an ability to handle himself when Rhonda took advantage of it.

My hope in presenting this account is to encourage couples who are experiencing problems to seek out professional help to reach true resolution of their problems.

Nadine Byrd

SESSION ONE

RHONDA PHONED FOR an appointment for herself and Jake. When I asked about the nature of the problem, her words were clipped. Her marriage "is on the rocks' and 'I doubt if I can hang on much longer."

That was Monday. I checked my appointments and saw a cancellation for Thursday at 11 AM. She said they would both come.

On Thursday a knock came on my door. I called, "Come in."

Rhonda came through the door first. She stomped in. It was difficult not to imagine a small elephant coming through the door. Her chin was up and the muscles in her jaw stood out like small burls on a tree trunk. Her fists were clenched. She seemed to wear her anger as if it were a beloved fur coat.

Jake followed. His coming surprised me. The rope around his neck pulling him in was nonexistent but nonetheless real. He came on short tripping steps with his head down. He was much taller than Rhonda; I judged him to be about 6' 2'. She was no more than 5' 6'. I had the impression I was looking at a teenaged boy instead of a man of 48 years.

The first session was the usual muddle. Rhonda's list of complaints against Jake seemed endless. Jake on his part was defensive. My experience told me Rhonda's list was likely accurate, but more importantly, the real problem was buried under Rhonda's Complaint Mountain.

I tried to get them to talk to each other without success. Rhonda would not look at Jake. He tried to talk to her, but she physically turned her back to him.

Toward the end of the hour I asked them both if they wanted to save their marriage. Jake was immediately affirmative. Rhonda would only say she wanted to if Jake would change.

SESSION TWO

WHEN THEY CAME the next week, I suggested they take a test. They both wanted to know what kind of test I had in mind. I told them it was a test to determine how they approached the problems in their marriage.

Rhonda clued in immediately. "You mean it's a test to find out if I'm just being childish, don't you? Well, I'm not, and I'm not the problem here. I read about counselors doing that. You can nix that one right now."

I explained that everyone approaches situations in life from different points of view and from different levels. And it helps me to know what some of those approaches are.

Rhonda bristled. "I'm no child!" she said through clenched teeth. She got up and walked out.

Jake stood, shrugged with his palms up as if to say, 'What can I do?' and went out after her.

SESSION THREE

A FEW WEEKS LATER, I received a phone call from Jake. He wanted to see me alone.

When he came in, I saw a completely different person. He stood full height as he walked in. His strides were relaxed and he looked at ease. He was dressed in a dark blue pin striped suit with a white shirt with vertical maroon stripes. His tie was pale rust with an off-white swirly design in the center. His thick, deep-brown hair was neatly trimmed and made his light brown eyes catch my attention. His square face fit perfectly with his physique. I couldn't help but gulp. I hope I concealed it. He gave no hint of noticing.

He sat. I moved from behind my desk to a chair angled toward his.

J: May I ask what you prefer to be called?

N: Certainly. My name is Nadine Byrd, as you know. You may call me Nadine.

J: Thank you. Well, Nadine, you said something when Rhonda and I were here that caught my attention. Really, it made a deep impression on me. You said that we all approach areas of our lives from different levels. I don't remember ever hearing that before.

But it made me look at myself. I'm beginning to see how true that is, but I'm sure I'll need help along the way. It will have to be just the two of us. Rhonda vowed after we were here that she'd never set foot in this place again. But I need to make some changes, okay?

N: (I nodded.) I'd be glad to help in any way that I can. First, would you review your life briefly? Start with your parental home.

J: Okay. Well, there was Mom and Dad and two of us kids. Karen was three years younger than I. She died suddenly in a gym class when she was fourteen. She had a heart condition no one knew about. Mom was devastated. As I look back, it affected their marriage a lot. Mom and Dad were never close, it seemed to me. Dad never expressed himself. He was sort of stoical. Mom was more emotional. I missed my little sister. She leaned on me and I often took her into my confidence.

Dad was never home a lot. His business took him away, but he was home most weekends. After Karen's death, Mom poured all her attention and affection on me. I have to say I was spoiled. Dad had a great income so we had no wants.

Mom saw to it that I had everything I needed. I got what I wanted, really. As I look back I have to say I didn't waste a lot. But I enjoyed getting expensive stuff, like clothes and other things for school, especially in college. It was generally stuff I needed, but good stuff. I didn't go for the trivial stuff.

I did well in school. I don't remember kindergarten much, but we had a male teacher in first grade. He was wonderful. He made learning fun. Learning new things for me was like eating candy. I just couldn't understand kids who didn't like school. I was at the head of the class in point averages from then on all the way through high school. College was even better than the lower grades. I excelled in my business courses. I found out the prof often used my papers in other classes as an example of how to do research and how to present it in written form.

I liked some sports, too. Basketball was my all-time favorite. I was on our high school and college teams. It was at one of our games that I saw Rhonda. She was from the other high school and dating a guy on that team. She caught my eye. When I finally met her, we hit it off quickly. We married the year after I graduated. She still had six months to go so I got a job in her town.

N: How did your marriage go?

J: The first six, eight months were good. But when she graduated things changed. I must honestly say my selfishness came out big time. I see that now. But I didn't see it then.

N: Can you fill that out a little?

J: Well, I was very demanding. I didn't know how to give.

N: Demanding?

J: Yeah. Like I wanted it to be like it was at home.

N: You wanted her to be like your mother?

J: Ouch! You're right. I didn't think of it like that. Yeah, I guess that's it. Pretty bad, huh?

N: Are you saying Rhonda didn't want to play Mama?

J: That's what she said, too. To me that wasn't normal; that was not being a wife.

N: A wife should spoil her husband?

J: Another ouch! Now that it's on the table like that, it doesn't look right at all. But, yes, that's what I assumed. Red flag! (He lifted his forefinger.) Changes are needed.

N: That's where you need to grow?

J: Yeah, I sure do. But at the same time I don't want to. It's painful looking backward.

N: Regrets?

J: A ton of them, now that I look at it.

N: Our time is up…

J: The time goes too fast here. Next week?

N: Yes. I'll see you in a week.

SESSION FOUR

JAKE BEGAN TALKING immediately on being seated.

J: You know, for the first time I started to look at my life as a whole and with honesty. I mean my business life and personal life at the same time. I was shocked at what I discovered.

There is a huge gap between my personal life and my business self. At my business I operate on a pretty good adult level. But the minute I step through the door at home I change. Really, I revert to a boy. Somehow I always felt something was going on but I could never pinpoint it. I blamed Rhonda a lot. But now I see it's actually me. I had a hard time admitting that, but in all honesty I can't avoid it any longer. That's what happens. I want…no, I need to change that. It made me feel sick. I wanted to hide from the truth and deny it, but I can't any longer, at least if I'm sincere about changing.

N: Jake, I'm impressed and pleased how far you've come in such a short time. You are unusual in making such progress so soon. What do you feel caused that?

J: Thanks. Well, as I said last week, I know I need to change, as painful as it may be. Another thing is Rhonda's being so close to divorce lit a fire under me. I'm disgusted with myself and I don't want to lose Rhonda.

N: A divorce would be painful?

J: Yes, but it's more than that. I really don't want to lose her. (Begins to cry) She has her faults but she means everything to me. (Sobs) I think she's already seen a lawyer. (He hangs his head.)

N: Does she know how you feel about her?

J: 'Thereby hangs the tale', to quote the Bard. (We laughed; Jake through his tears.)

N: How do you mean that?

J: We don't talk anymore. If I try she just shouts me down and shuts me out. All she says is that I'm trying to buy my way back into bed with her and that will never happen, so she tells me to just shut the h— up. We sleep in separate rooms. Have for years now. We just happen to live in the same house, that's all our marriage is, two people, married, living in the same house.

N: Are you trying to buy your way back?

J: Uh. Yes and no. What I mean is that I don't just want to be in bed with her. I want to get back to a real marriage. (Weeps openly)

N: (after he stops) And you don't know how to do that?

J: Bingo and bull's eye. You're right. Nothing I've done has worked. That's why I'm here, I guess.

N: I gather you've tried to convince her that you'll be a different person if she'd just give you a chance?

J: Gosh. It's like you've been living in our house. (We laugh) She just won't listen. I'm shot down before I get off the ground.

N: Jake, (he looks up at me) the bad news is you'll never be able to convince her…

J: You're telling me it's hopeless? I can't hear that. There has to be a way.

N: That road is closed, Jake.

J: Then what's left? Do I just give up? I can't do that.

N: You think about it. We'll explore that next week.

J: I see. Two tickets to next week's production. (We laugh) I have no idea where that saying comes from but Dad used to say that when something was unfinished. Same time and place?

I nodded and he left.

SESSION FIVE

J: BOY, I DIDN'T know a little idea could occupy so much of my mind and time. Where we ended last time really tied me up. The conclusion I came up with is that if I can't convince Rhonda, I have to convince myself.

N: And you are convinced, is that it?

J: Yes. I'm certain. I know I've changed. You can see that, too, can't you?

N: What makes you so certain?

J: I just know I'll be different. I mean, I know I am different.

N: You have proof?

J: What do you mean? Can't a person be sure?

N: Certainly. You're ready for all the bumps or roadblocks, I take it.

J: Oh, I guess you're right. What proof do I have, really? Just saying I know is not enough. So I'm back to square one. And I'm lost.

N: Perhaps, but I suggest you turn around.

J: What do you mean, turn around? I think I am.

N: Who are you trying to convince?

J: Rhonda, of course.

N: When you're not convinced yourself?

J: Oh my word. You're right again. So the answer is to convince myself without reference to Rhonda. Oh, that's what you mean by turning around? Face myself. Just prove to myself I'm different. The question is how do I do that?

N: We'll talk about that next time.

J: Those hours go by too quickly … I'll see you next week.

SESSION SIX

N: HOW WAS the week, Jake?

J: Ponderous. (Laughter) I mean pondering, of course. But it was ponderous, too.

N: Did you come to any conclusions?

J: Well, if I need to face myself and prove to myself I'm different, then I have to make changes and keep them. It means to be more adult in how I act at home. And I keep reminding myself I have to keep Rhonda out of the picture. Just do it because I want and need to do it and to stick with it no matter what.

N: That, to you, is being more adult?

J: Yes. And part of that means to take on responsibility. I saw a big, no huge gap between my professional self and my personal self. I take on responsibility professionally but not personally. We talked about that before.

N: What made the gap? Any ideas?

J: I've thought about that. Why? Well, it's embarrassing, but for me it is because I want to stay a little boy when I'm at home. An irresponsible little boy. And I came to a big conclusion.

N: That sounds interesting.

J: It wasn't easy. I have to push Mom out the back door or the front door, whatever. I have to get her out of the house.

N: You have to reject your mother?

J: That's what it seemed like at first, but not really. I just have to admit that she was wrong in what she did and I am wrong to want to keep it up. She wanted me to stay her little boy forever. She said that and I bought it. I'm the one who needs to change it. I just now had a thought. Hmm. I need to kick the little boy out the door with my mother. They both have to go. Well, well – But I've run into a problem I don't know how to deal with.

N: How do you see that? What's the problem as you see it?

J: Well, you see, Rhonda gets together with a few friends regularly. They go out to lunch and sometimes dinner together.

N: That's a problem for you?

J: Oh. No, no. That's no problem at all. She needs her friends. It's fine by me. But the other night, Kitty, one of them invited the others and their mates to her house for cocktails. There were a few other couples there, too. They do that with each other. This Kitty pulls me aside into their spare bedroom. To be honest, I don't like her. Actually she repulses me. Well, she said, 'Jake, Rhonda tells us she sees the changes you're making and she says she knows it's because you want to get into bed with her again. And that's never going to happen.' What a kick in the groin, huh?'

N: How did you deal with that?

J: I would like to have spit her in the eye. I was angry and sick to my stomach at the very idea which I knew she had in mind. I said, 'Kitty, if Rhonda says something to you in your group, keep it to yourself. I don't want to hear about it.'

N: How did Kitty take that?'

J: Well, I just stood there looking her straight in the face. She blushed and said, 'I was just trying to be helpful.' Before she could turn around I said, 'Kitty, that was not helpful at all. Please, go put your underwear back on. I'm not going to bed with you.'

N: Wise response, Jake.

J: To be honest, I felt a little guilty. I hurt her, but at the same time I couldn't let her get by with that. She was too far out of line, even if she was hostess.

But, she was right in a way. She touched on a problem between me and Rhonda. Rhonda sees the changes I'm making, of course, and I can tell she's getting angrier all the time. She's avoiding me even more.

N: Does that bother you?

J: Not really. It's only more of the same, in a way. But the boiler is going to blow some time and likely sooner than later. I don't know what I'll do. She's going to throw her feelings in my face, I know it. She always does and I have never handled it right. I guess I'm scared.

N: Let's go back a little. Why are you making the changes, Jake?

J: To prove to myself I can be different. I can grow. I can mature.

N: Isn't that your answer? But our time is up.

J: Two more of those tickets. (Laughter) But it will have to be three weeks from today. Business reasons.

N: Fine. I'll see you in three weeks.

SESSION SEVEN

J: WELL, WHAT A time that was. The steam escaped, but only partly, I think.

N: Can you talk about it?

J: Sure. It's a long story. I was working the back lawn when she came home one day. She came storming out of the garage with her fists on her hips. 'We have to talk.' So I laid my tools down and walked her to the tool shed.

'I know what you're doing and so do you,' she said. I played dumb. 'I don't know what you mean, and I won't play that game. So unless you say what you mean, this conversation is over and I'm going back to work.' I turned to leave. She hollered, 'Don't you dare walk away from me, Mr.' I said, 'Oh, I dare and I will unless you say what you mean and I won't give you a third chance.'

I was angry. I stopped for a minute and then turned and started to walk out. Before I got to the door she shouted, 'I mean we both know you're just trying to buy your way back into my bed. It's not going to work!'

'Oh. Okay. May I be allowed to respond to that?' She just stood there with her arms folded. I looked at her. 'I guess,' she finally said. So I said, 'Rhonda, I know and accept that we'll never share a bed again. I bear full responsibility for that. The way I acted and the hurt I inflicted on you by my self-centeredness, my stupid childish egomania could only lead to that. I regret that. There's not a day goes by that I don't regret what I did to you, the pain I gave you. So what I'm doing is not trying to earn anything.'

'Then what…'

I interrupted her. 'Just because I know I ruined any chance of physical intimacy between us doesn't mean I shouldn't change for myself. I've come to hate myself for what I've been and I'm making some changes because of that and that only. I'm not trying to get back into bed with you and hurt you some more. I have a very childish side and I want to grow up and be a responsible adult. That's what I'm doing here and that's all I'm doing.'

I was shaking like a leaf in a stiff breeze when I finished. It wasn't a planned thing at all. I'd been thinking about it, sure, but that's just the way it came out.

N: Jake, you amaze me. How did Rhonda react?

J: She just stood there with nothing to say. Really, it looked like the wind went out of her sails. I walked out and went back to my trimming. I wonder what your reaction is to what I said.

N: Better still is your evaluation of it. How do you feel about what you said?

J: It's such new ground for me. I tried to stay calm and suppress my anger. I've never tried to do anything like that before, stand up to her I mean and not shout and scream. As I said, she was speechless for a change. I may still have to face divorce, but I'll deal with that if and when it comes. All in all, I think I faced myself for the first time in my life, too. I found out I'm not as helpless as I thought. Yet, it scares me a little. What if I pushed Rhonda over the edge?

N: To compliment yourself is the greatest compliment of all. It's a person like yourself that makes me want to go on. And I don't think you'll have to worry about Rhonda.

J: I sincerely hope not. That would be an awful, terrible, horrible, no good, very bad day, to quote little Andrew.

N: Jake, have you thought about where we go from here?

J: Somehow I expected you would ask that. I feel I can make if on my own for a while, at least. I'd like to try. I suppose at some point I'll need to come back, I think. Rhonda and I are going to have a tete-a-tete sometime in the near future. I'll likely need to come back then.

SESSION EIGHT

JAKE ASKED FOR a session some two months later. He sat down but didn't look at me or say anything. I felt he needed the quiet. I waited. After nearly five minutes he looked up at me.

J: Thank you, Nadine. I needed the quiet. I needed to get composed.

N: You're welcome.

J: The pot's on the stove and boiling hard. I wish something would happen. I don't know how much longer I can see it boil without doing something. I know what I have to do. Do you remember that little book you gave me, *Little Pot Boil?* (I nodded.) It could have been written about us, about me.

Well, the book says the person who is boiling the pot wants the other person to do something about it. That's why they're letting it boil. That's dangerous. Don't do it. There's three things a person may be tempted to do.

The first is to take the pot off the fire. Watch out. You have let the other person's anger hook yours. You are bound to get scalded because the pot is going to tip on you. It's a premature act and only delays any chance of real resolution.

The second temptation is to somehow try to put out the fire. That's even worse. It is saying the other person has no right to their anger. While that may or may not be true the other person will not accept that at all. The third temptation is to take the other person away from the pot. That is treating the other person like a child. The pot will explode all over.

The answer is to wait. At some point you may be able to say, 'It seems to me you're angry. When you're ready to talk about it calmly, I'm willing to listen.'

Well, I did and that's why I'm here.

N: Something happened you didn't expect?

J: And how! She said, 'There you go, you high and mighty jerk.

You think you're so much better than the rest of us you stink. You think you're so superior you can look down your stupid nose at the rest of mankind. You're nothing but s— under my feet. The quicker I can clean you off me the better I'll be.'

N: That shocked you?

J: I stood there stunned. A kick in the groin or a slap upside the head would have been easier to take. But she surprised me by staying standing there. After a while I said as calmly as I could, 'No, Rhonda, I'm not better than you, but neither am I going to fight with you.' As I walked out she said, 'Well, you've become human after all.' I guess I don't get it.

N: You don't know what you are dealing with?

J: No, I don't. That's why I'm here.

N: What's Rhonda feeling, do you think?

J: Well, she sees the changes I'm making. I believe she doesn't like it. I don't know why.

N: How did you feel about her attack?

J: It hurt. I was angry but blowing up never helped and won't now. Somewhere I read or heard a soft answer turns anger away. So I tried the soft answer. But I don't get the thing about becoming human.

N: Where did Rhonda think you were sitting?

J: On some pedestal somewhere.

N: Do you feel she sensed your anger?

J: Oh. Yes. Now I get it. She knew I was angry but in the end I wouldn't fight. So I'm off the pedestal, at least for now.

N: Do you feel she would like the old Jake back?

J: I don't think so. But I feel she's testing me at the same time. Am I going to blow the way I always did when she lit into me? I think she wants me to blow and at the same not do it. It's confusing.

N: You're saying you've taken away her reason to be angry at you?

J: Yeah, you're right! Maybe the put down is just trying to see how real I am. Am I going to get angry at her? The problem is I might in a weak moment do just that. Then what? I hate to think about it. I guess I need to be really strong and not let her get to me.

N: You want to answer her without stomping on her?

J: For sure. That would be the worst thing I could do. There were times I wanted to lash out. But that would just be repeating the past childishness. I can't let that happen.

N: I hear you saying you don't want to put a pot on the stove with her?

J: That's good. Let her cook up whatever she wants to. But I don't want to be vindictive about it either. I just don't want to hurt her some more. Thanks, Nadine. I see the time is up. I'll phone you if I need to.

N: Any time, Jake. My door is always open.

SESSION NINE

RHONDA PHONED asking to meet with me. Her anger on her coming was palpable.

R: I guess you know I vowed never to set foot in this place again. (I waited.) Well, I guess I'm here to set the record straight. I'm sure the idiot has painted a pretty black picture of me, huh? (I waited.) You just as well agree because I know it's true.

N: Rhonda, if you're so sure it's true, I wonder why you're here?

R: Oh, there you go with your pretty non-answers. But I'll get the truth out of you one way or another.

N: Do you want me to fight with you, Rhonda?

R: Why can't you talk like a real human being? (About three minutes of silence) Okay, just sit there on your high and mighty throne and feel superior. I guess here's where Jake learned it. You sit here plotting together how you can look down your noses and the rest of the world. (Silence) Well?

N: May I ask you a question? (She nods slightly) What does Jake do to make you feel he's acting superior?

R: Humph. It isn't anything specific. I just know that is what he is feeling. I know you are, too. It shows all over you. I can tell. I wasn't born yesterday.

N: You're quite angry at Jake, and me as well?

R: Who wouldn't be! Anyone would be furious at such airs of superiority.

N: You seem determined to remain angry.

R: And how. Until the two of you get off your high and mighty thrones.

N: How will you determine I'm off this throne?

R: When you talk and act normal like the rest of us.

N: Do you mean when I'll get angry and fight with you?

R: Well, at least you'd be a little more human.

N: How do you feel getting angry and fighting is more human?

R: Well, it just is.

(Silence)

N: Rhonda, is it that you know how to deal with an angry person but you don't know how to deal with someone who won't get angry?

R: There you go again, making me feel inferior.

N: If I would get angry, you would feel like the winner?

R: I don't know. I just can't deal with this any longer. I don't know why I came. I should have known you'd just sit there on your throne.

She leaves.

SESSION TEN

THREE WEEKS LATER Rhonda phoned for an appointment. She came in and sat.

R: Okay. You can go ahead and feel like the winner. You got me.

N: How so?

R: You should know. Don't you know how everyone feels? (Silence) Okay? You said I know how to deal with an angry person but not when they won't get angry.

N: Jake won't get angry anymore and you don't know how to deal with that?

R: Well, that's what you told me.

N: I remember it as a question.

R: What's the difference?

N: To you there's no difference?

R: Well, maybe, I guess. (Silence) Well, okay. One is telling me how I feel and the other is asking how I feel ...Oh, I see. You want to throw it back on me. You want me to tell you my feelings so then you can use them against me. Maybe that works with Jake. It won't work with me.

N: Do you feel you need to defend yourself against me?

R: And how. I sure do.

N: I'm a dangerous person?

R: (She laughs) Yes and no. I guess you wouldn't purposely hurt anyone. But you sure upset the old apple cart at our house. Jake is just as impossible as you are. If I get rid of the bum it will be your fault.

N: As you see it, how will it be my fault?

R: It just will be. Look at what's happened. Jake is...well, he's changed and...oh, I don't know.

N: Rhonda. (She looks at me.) Will you do something a moment?

R: I guess.

N: Would you review why you made the first phone call and what brings you here now?

R: (Pauses and then begins to cry. I gave her the box of tissues.) I was fed up with Jake. I was fed up with marriage. I was going to call it quits, but a couple of good friends of mine told me that no matter what I did, I needed to get help. She recommended you as the best and made me agree to try.

(She sobs.) I came because I knew you'd agree with me that Jake was hopeless. And then something got him started seeing you. And now he's (through sobs) being so different. I'm always picking fights with him and he won't fight any more. When I start screaming and yelling at him, he just stands there a while. Then he'll say something like, 'If we can't talk our problems out like two adults, I think I want to go back to my work' or whatever it is he's doing then. I want to punch him. I want to kick him, but I know he's right. Why do I do that?

N: Things went very differently than you expected?

R: And how! You want to know what he did awhile back? I am sure he's changing just to get back in bed with me. I won't have it. So I accused him of that. You know what he did? He calmly stood there and took all the blame for the situation we're in. He said he was totally sick of himself for being such a jerk and an egomaniac. He said he was not trying to get back in bed with me. He knew he had ruined that for good by the hurt and abuse he inflicted on me. He said he's changing just so he can live with himself and stop hurting me. I want to believe him but I don't know if I can.

N: Do you feel a little lost?

R: (Her head comes up. She puts a hand to her mouth.) Lost? Yes, I do.

N: Would you like to find your way back?

R: Yes, but I'm scared.

N: Afraid? Of what?

R: Of you. (I look at her and raise my eyebrows.) I'm scared you'll read me the riot act for the way I am. But I guess you won't do that. (Silence) No. I guess I'm scared of myself. Scared of what I might find. Scared of my anger. Oh, I'm so ashamed. (She cries for a time.) And so confused.

N: I understand. However, our time is up for now, Rhonda.

R: Okay. I need to come back if I may.

N: You certainly may. We can make next week if you wish. (She nods and leaves.)

SESSION ELEVEN

R: WELL, I'M BACK.

N: That's not so easy for you?

R: It isn't so easy. It makes me eat humble pie.

N: I understand. Rhonda. But I'm wondering if you'll do something? Would you be willing to give me brief review of your life? Begin with parental home, if you will.

R: Sure. I can do that. (I see her relax.) Well, there was Mom and Daddy, of course. Daryll was the oldest, then me. We were a little over a year and a half apart. We were always close.

Daryll was the best brother a sister could have. He looked after me and made me always feel safe, right from the time I started school. I was somewhat of a scaredy-cat. Lila was five years younger than I. We call her Sissy. Buddy, that's Frank, was over three years younger than Sissy. He was a long time being born and has some developmental issues. He does well but will never be like other adults.

N: How did you relate to one another at home?

R: Hmm. (takes a few moments) Probably the best I can do is tell you a story. It was when Daryll was a junior in high school … Well, let me go back. Daddy was always kinda quiet, but he was a good father. Daryll and I loved him. He was like a rock. We lived in a new development. Our row of houses was on the edge of a big field which was behind us. Daddy helped Daryll and the other boys make a big playing area there. He helped the boys clear the area and mow it. In return the guys often mowed our lawn, which was big. All the kids played on that field. It was nice. Well, one night we were at dinner.

N: This was when Daryll…

R: Oh, yes. Daryll was a junior. Mom was always a yeller. She'd yell about everything. She yelled at us kids. She yelled at Daddy. She never up to that time spoke two calm words together that I can recall. She was yelling at Daddy for being such a jerk and dumbbell and lots of other bad names for wasting time on that field and wearing out our mower and such. It was embarrassing.

Well, Daryll butted in and said, 'Mom, why do you always have to yell at Dad? All the guys think I've got the greatest dad in the world, and I do too. We can play back there and not have to worry about cars in the street or hitting little kids or busting windows. Why do you always have to yell about it? All the guys help mow our lawn with their mowers and he helps us. When he can, he umps our games and it's great…'

Daddy stopped him and said, 'Son, you shouldn't talk to your mother that way. Come with me.' He got up and went to the boy's bedroom. We heard them talking a while and then we heard three big whomps. Nobody was eating. Mom went to the sink. I didn't look at her but I know she was crying. Sissy started crying.

When Daddy came out he was limping and said, 'Son, when you're ready, you come finish your dinner.' He picked up Sissy and comforted her. He said, 'I know you're hurting and that's OK.' He looked at me. 'Daryll is a big boy. He'll be fine. Sometimes daddies have to do hard things.' He kissed her and smoothed back here hair. You better eat now, Pumpkin Seed.' She jumped down and said, 'Plant one on you,' and punched his arm a little. He acted real hurt and said, 'Now you'll have to cover me with dirt to make it grow,' as he held his arm. They always did that. It was funny. She laughed and ate the rest of her dinner. Daryll came to the table but didn't eat much. Daddy excused him and he went back into his room.

I wanted to go hug Daryll and comfort him. I was kinda mad at Daddy.

The next day we were waiting for the bus. Daryll said, 'I'll tell you a secret if you double five not to tell anyone, ever.' Double five is like saying you'll go the hell if you break the promise. I knew it was serious so I did a double five on his arm. It's like putting both hands on the Bible. Then he told me Daddy didn't hit him at all. He told Daryll he was proud of him for standing up for something he thought was right. Daryll was becoming a man which made Daddy proud. Oh, he needed to learn to do it better, but he was still proud of his son and always would be.

Daryll wanted to know why Daddy didn't do something. 'OK, son. You're getting to be a man. What would you do in my place? ...You see? Okay. Now let me say something man to man. Your mother has a problem, but she still deserves our respect even though she can't control her mouth.' Then he hit himself on his bad thigh three times. You see, Daddy was hit on a crosswalk by a drunk driver when he was younger. He said, 'Think it over, son. You'll understand why I made you go to your room.'

I could hardly believe that about Daddy. He hit himself. That's why he came out of the room limping a little. It did make me see him differently and Mom, too. She didn't yell so much after that. When she did, she'd look at Daryll and then stop.

Daryll was really smart. He was the best. But after that he was even better. All the kids looked up to him. He wouldn't let anyone pester me or anyone else. One time a kid was mocking another kid who had a limp. Daryll made that kid take one shoe off and run around the whole recess with one shoe off. That kid was crying, but he never mocked anybody again.

Everybody learned that Daryll wouldn't put up with that stuff. Some guys were making fun of Daryll once. He went up to them and said, 'So what would you like to do about it, huh?' He took a step and those kids ran like scared bunnies.

He was a real leader, but he never acted proud about it. He never became a bossy jerk.

Well, Daryll went on to become a lawyer. He's a successful one, too. He helps out Mom and Daddy all the time and sees to it they have no needs. We talk on the phone at least once a week. He told me he is what he is because of that incident in his bedroom.

N: Rhonda? Excuse me, do you mean Daryll Franzjes is your

brother, *the* Daryll Franzjes?

R: Yes, *the* Daryll Franzjes is my big brother. And I'm proud of him.

N: That's wonderful. But, Rhonda, do you see any parallels between yourself and your home life?

R: (Looks at me. Tears form in her eyes) Oh, dear. I never saw it before. I'm a yeller like my mother. I swore I'd never be like that, but I am. I guess I told myself I have reasons. Mom didn't.

N: And you wanted Jake to be like your father, or perhaps your brother?

R: Oh dear! You have a way of seeing right through me. Really, I guess, I need to let Jake be Jake. And since he's been talking to you, he's never done one mean thing to me. It's just the opposite. He's kind and I'm the mean one.

From this point on I will continue in story form as Rhonda gave it to me in our sessions. When she began to trust me she needed to tell me everything. It was in doing so she found a great deal of healing. She could tell it all without fearing repercussion. I began to feel there was something deep in Rhonda's life that had a big influence on her. Much later she revealed it.

R: I learned from counselling that I had a lot of pent-up anger. It was mostly directed at Jake for all the ways he hurt me. I wouldn't let it go. I learned my anger was also a revenge. I carried a deep need to get back at Jake. I needed the payback.

At the same time, I wanted to carry the hurt I felt like a badge of honor. And that was self-pity. I started to be disgusted with myself. But I thought Jake was sitting on a pedestal looking down his nose at me. So I devised what I thought was a brilliant plan. It would prove me right. I was sure of it. Then I'd kick him out of my life forever. That would get rid of the hurt, too, at least so I thought. I was in for a surprise.

It was a Thursday. Thursdays are always half-days for him, so I knew he'd be home when I got there about four. I expected him to be loafing around or sleeping. He was going to get my car serviced like he always did. To my surprise he was in the back yard raking and cleaning up. I was as angry as a charging bull. I worked it up all the way home. So I came out of the garage and marched up to him. He saw me coming and stopped raking. Oh, was I mad!

I put my fists on my hips, 'Jake, will you do something for me?'

'Sure, just name it. If I can it's yours.'

'Will you kiss me?'

His mouth went open. He didn't say a word. You see, that was my brilliant plan. If he refused to kiss me I'd know he was on a pedestal and our marriage was over. If he just gave me a peck on the cheek, it was the same. Curtains on this sham marriage. It was going to be one or the other, I just knew it. I didn't see any other possibility. Only I didn't count on the new Jake.

What does Jake do? He turned around and tossed the rake away. He came up to me, put his hands on my shoulders and looked me in the eyes. I'll never forget that soft loving look in his eyes. He seemed to be asking, 'Do you really want this?' Then he drew me into his arms. His left arm was over my shoulders. He lifted my chin with it. His right one was on my waist and pulling me to him. Then he kissed me with the softest, most loving, wonderful kiss I ever remember getting. I had all I could do to keep from wetting myself, I was in such shock.

I noticed he was hard as a rock. I pushed my hip against it a little. It was so wonderful. I was tingling like never before. He held me by the shoulders afterward and laid a cheek against mine and said softly in my ear, 'Rhonda, I can't control that. It just happens. It was not a request.'

He went to get my car serviced. I just stood there. Never did I expect a kiss like that. My trap snapped on me. Now what? All of a sudden I realized what his remark meant. He thought I was pushing against him to say, 'Get rid of it, Buster, and stop dreaming!' It broke my heart. What else could he think? I came up to him mad as a hornet with enough poison to kill him on the spot! I ran to my bedroom and bawled and bawled like never before. I screamed. I didn't think I could stop, but by the time he came home the hiccups were gone and I had a dinner of sorts ready. In the past he would have told me off and then gone to the diner to eat. But he ate as if he enjoyed every bite.

Crazy me. I was not done with him yet. My mind went to the next step I had planned. I made him go into the family room while I cleaned up. I told him I needed to talk to him. When I went into the family room, he immediately laid the paper down. Our couch and a companion chair are at right angles to each other with a table in the angle of the two. He patted the couch next to him. I shook my head and sat in the chair.

'Jake, I need to know something once and for all.'

'Sure, what is it?'

'Well, I need to know. Right now. Are you keeping another woman?'

He looked at me with his brow furrowed. Silence. I knew then I had him cornered. 'Well, you said "keeping." Truthfully, Rhonda. Yes, I am.'

I was blown away. 'You admit it finally? When were you going to tell me?'

'As soon as I felt you would listen to me.'

'Well, I'm listening. At least I want to know her name. And it better not be a friend.'

'Actually, it isn't one, it's three. And you know them all.'

I fell back in my chair dumbfounded. 'Three? Isn't one good enough? You have to have three? OK, I'll skip the bad words I'd like to say. You're going to name them for me and right now!'

'Sure. First, it's your mother.'

'My mother! What? Oh. You're paying for my mother's care? I told you, Big-time Jerk, I told you I don't want you doing that. That's my brother's job, you spineless idiot. You're letting him off the hook, you stupid dope.'

'Rhonda, I'm not letting him off the hook. Daryll wanted to

pay it all. He finally agreed to let me pay half the cost of living at the home. He's taking care of all the rest. Her clothes, medicines, personals and sundries. Remember, she's your mother, too. I couldn't in good conscience let him do everything. I wanted to tell you, but …'

'OK. Well, I guess I see your point but that's only one. You really have another?'

Silence. I knew I had him for sure.

'Jennine.'

'Our daughter? You know how I feel about that, too, Jake the Jerk.'

'I know.'

'So that's why you didn't tell me, is it?'

'Yes, Rhonda. I was sure you'd think I was begging. I'm not and she can't do it all alone … Yes, I know what you want to say, but, as long as I can afford it I'm not going to let her pile up debts. She's our daughter. I love her. I had to make a choice. If you think I'm wrong, I'm wrong!'

'OK. Let's get it over with! Number three!'

'It's you. You're number three, but you're really number one.'

'Me? What do you mean, me? Of course you're supporting me and the whole house.'

'But that's not what I mean … Just let me tell you, OK? You know my income is solely from commissions. I don't get a salary, really. I earn my own pay by what I do for the company. That means I won't get a pension. I have to put money aside for that. I've been doing that from day one. But I'm putting some aside just for you. It's your account. I've done it all legally through a lawyer. You're worth close to a half mil. And it's tax free, except for the interest it accrues. That's what I'm doing for you.'

'Half a million! How can you afford it? Jake, you're too much. You never told me …Yeah, it's because you know what I'd say and you were right, you jerk. Just how can you afford it? But, before you tell me, I have a question. Why have you cut off

Mackenzie from your support? He needs to know his father is standing behind him and loves him, don't you think?

'OK. I can answer that. I haven't cut him off really. I keep in contact with him and let him know I love him. But my love will not support his lifestyle. I won't give him money to waste on drinking and partying. When he wants to get serious about his education, I'll give him all he needs.

By the way, I've put in a special account every cent I would have given him the last three plus years. When he buckles down, it will all be his instantly. I have asked Jennine to stop giving him money, too. I know you give him money and I don't want to control what you do with your money, but I won't waste mine on him.

'The answer to your other question is that I'm well up in the six figure bracket in income from my company. I'm top man in the company for bringing in clients. I have been since my third year with them. If things keep going the way they are now, in a couple of years I'll be in the one million bracket. I'll be the first in the company to do that. The problem is the company's policy. They will allow that for three years and then I'm out. I'll have to do something else. I agreed to not do the same thing on my own for the next three years after that. It's all in the contract I signed.'

'A million in one year? Heavens, that's almost too much to believe. Just what do you do anyway? I could never figure it out.'

'We help struggling businesses get back on their feet. I've been very successful in finding clients and keeping them through the whole process of their recovery. I've done so well that many struggling companies have been contacting me for help. They're even coming from north of the border recently. I haven't had to go on the road for a long time, they come to me. We get various commissions for getting clients and keeping them. I can't go into it all. Besides the commissions, I have lots of stock in the company and that's growing real well now since the company is, too.'

'I guess I never listened before, did I? You take my breath away.'

'Before you stop breathing, I have something I want to give you, if you'll wait a minute.' (He went to his office and came back with a manila envelope.)

'What's that?'

'It's for you. Before you open it, though, I'd like to say something.' He looked at me and I shrugged my shoulders. 'You see, it's some money. I've waited until I thought the time was right to give it to you. You've always said you'd like to go on a cruise. I know we can't do that together, it wouldn't work. That doesn't mean, though, you can't have some fun. So open it and then I'd like to give you my suggestion what to do with it.'

I opened it and a whole lot of bills fell into my lap. He told me to count it. It came to thirty thousand dollars. I gasped. I was speechless. I just looked at him dumbstruck. Totally.

He smiled and said, 'Rhonda, I've been saving that up. Here's my suggestion. I'm taking two weeks' vacation the end of September. Take your two best friends and go on a cruise. I've arranged for a couple of buddies in the decorating business to come and do some painting and decorating here in the house. I know what you want … And I know what you're thinking. It's too much, but no, it isn't. Have fun and don't hold back. There's enough there for the three of you to have a good time for two or three weeks. You deserve it. And I don't want any money to come back.'

I ran to my bedroom and bawled again for a long time. I guess Jake knew he couldn't come to me. I took the next few days off from work. I bawled every time I even thought about that envelope.

I learned in counseling that I was having mixed feelings, a truck load of them. I was angry at Jake for changing. In a way I wanted him to stay the same. Then I had a right to be angry. Now I don't and that is making me feel guilty as can be. Also, I didn't want to change but I knew I had to. I am very revengeful and want to hurt Jake. It's deliberate, that's the sick part of it all. It's hard not to hate myself. I'm beginning to see what Jake meant about being sick of yourself for what you are.

At this point Nadine asked me to go back to the kiss I asked Jake to give me and why I cried afterward. She helped me see that I felt Jake's love for me, but I was not about to admit it. I was too consumed with my revenge. Because of that I wanted to hide behind the abuse of long ago. She helped me see that hating myself was no help at all. What I should focus on was growing into a better person. I'm trying.

After he gave me that money, Liz, Joan, and I met for lunch on Tuesday like usual. They came in together. They both looked at the envelope on the table.

'Rhonda, what's wrong. You look terrible. Don't tell us you're going through with a divorce!'

I shook my head. 'No. Sit down. You're both going to get the shock of your lives.'

Liz: 'Well, don't keep us waiting.' (I had ordered drinks. They came. We told the waiter we'd order later.)

R: Last Wednesday night I decided I was going to get an answer once and for all. So I asked Jake if he was keeping a woman on the side. You know what he said? (Two heads shook no.) With a twinkle in his eye he said not one but three.

J/L: Three? You mean it?

R: Yes. To make a long story short they were Mom, Jennine, and me.

L: You? Your mom and daughter I understand. But you?

R: Yes, Liz, me. He told me that he has been saving for my future from the time he started with the company. That's more than eighteen years. But the unbelievable is the amount.

L/J: Well, tell us already.

R: About a half mil.

J: You mean that? This brainless husband of yours?

R: Yes, and I'm beginning to see how brainless I am. The next thing he did really came out of the blue. He gave me this envelope. Open it, Joan. Go ahead and the two of you count it.

(They count) J/L: Thirty thousand dollars. What ...

R: He said he knew how much I'd like to go on a cruise. He knew it wouldn't work for us to go together. So he told me to take my two best friends and enjoy a good two-week cruise. All, I mean *all* expenses paid. Trip, side trips, souvies, clothes, anything. All paid. He doesn't want us to come back with one red cent, he said.

J: Did he mean us two with you?

R: Yes, Joan, he meant the two of you.

J: What about Kitty. I know she's ...

L: 'Xcuse me, Joan. I think I just realized something. Oh, migosh (her hands go to her mouth.) Do you remember that cocktail party that Kitty threw for all of us? (Heads nod.) Well, I was coming out of the bathroom. I saw Kitty drag Jake around the corner into her spare bedroom. I should have gone on but I'm glad I stayed. Kitty said, 'Jake...

R: Oh, no!

L: Hold on, Rhonda. She said, 'Jake, Rhonda sees the changes you're making but she thinks you're just trying to get back in bed with her. What a kick in the groin, huh?' She started to say, 'I know how much a man needs...' but Jake cut her off. He said, 'Kitty, if Rhonda says something to your group, you keep it to yourself. I don't want to know about it.' Jake just stood there and Kitty said, 'I was just trying to be helpful.' Jake said, 'Kitty, that was not helpful at all.' Now listen to the rest of it. I about fell over. He said, 'Kitty, please go put your underwear back on. I'm not going to bed with you!' I nearly whooped. I ran back to the bathroom to laugh it off in a towel. I wanted to hug Jake for the best comeback I've ever heard in my entire life.

J: That really happened?

L: I lie not. I give it to you word for word.

R: Liz, you just helped me understand something. Jake thinks Kitty is a total airhead. That night Jake came to me early and said he needed to get home fast. On the way to the car he gave me the keys. He told me to stop as we came up to the garage. He got out and started throwing up. He retched. I got a glass of water. He rinsed, then drank part of it and threw that up, too. I asked but he told me it wasn't the food, but don't ask. I had to let it go. Now I know what happened. That's why he doesn't want Kitty along with us. (crying) I didn't know. My Jake! Forgive me!

J: It's OK, Rhonda. (whispering) Don't look now, but talk about the devil.

K: Hi, you three. What's going on? Looks like secrets going around.

L: You're right. Sit down, we have some wonderful news. We're going on a cruise.

K: All four of us? That's great news. When and where?

R: No, Kitty. Just the three of us. You're not included.

K: What? Why am I excluded? I know I haven't been here often lately, but I still want to be part of the gang. I had things pressing and couldn't always make it. I wanted to be here.

J: We're sure you did, but that's not the reason at all why you're excluded.

L: Don't start, Kitty. It's for a very special reason. You see, Jake is giving us the cruise.

K: What? Why is he excluding me? What's this special reason?

L: Kitty, let's be honest. We just realized why you threw that cocktail party at your house.

K: What do you mean? I wanted …

L: Spare us, Kitty. Spare us. I happened to hear you talking to Jake that night. And, no, I was not eavesdropping. I just came out of the bathroom at the right time. Do you want me to repeat what was said there? No, I didn't think so. You expected Jake to run with you to your bed. You thought he couldn't possibly resist your unbelievable charm. You had your guest room all set and ready … Yes, Kitty, I saw it. The blankets turned back and the perfume? … It stank to high heaven. Do you want to know what Jake did right after? He left the party with Rhonda and went home. He threw up like he couldn't stop when he got home.

K: Well, his stomach was upset. He told me …

R: A lie, Kitty. A bald-faced lie. He said nothing more to you and you know it. I asked him if it was the food. He said it wasn't but don't ask him what. Thanks to Liz, now I know. He does not deal well with too much perfume and scents. They make him ill. You can leave any time and we'll all be far better off.

K: Well, it was just a little mistake …

J: No! Kitty, it was not just a little mistake. Stop lying to yourself and us. It was the most juvenile, stupid, idiotic, half-assed, mean-spirited blunder you could ever have made. You betrayed our trust. You took advantage of us all. But what you did to Rhonda is completely unforgiveable and don't try to fool yourself anymore. You will never be welcome in this group again. So please do not order anything. If you do the rest of us will leave the restaurant.

K: Humph! You insignificant twits aren't worthy of my company …

R: Oh, we know that. You're so far above us we'll never be able to see you up in your clouds. (laughter. Kitty stomps out with her nose in the air.)

L: Good, Rhonda. That was a precious comeback.

The friends went on to plan their cruise. They never had such fun. And Rhonda came back to a beautifully decorated house. The interior decorator made it look like a totally new home, to quote Rhonda.

R: With my counselor's gentle but firm help, I was coming to grips with my anger and desire for revenge. It was so painful. I shed more tears in a few months than I thought I could make in a few years. I thought my anger was so justified … Well, actually I learned that anger is justified in the face of abuse, but the acting

130

out as I did is not. And did I ever act out. I took every chance I got to cut Jake down and hurt him. He deserved it. The crazy thing was as Jake changed I became more and more unhappy and more abusive.

My counselor helped me see I was unhappy with myself and deeply jealous of him. I wanted to 'kill' him for being so much better than I. As I look back I can see how hard I fought against changing. I had to overcome my fear of the guilt feelings that I knew would need to admit. When I did that, with a lot of kindly help, I could admit my abusiveness of Jake was worse than his of me. Mine was planned, deliberate and methodically carried out. His was not excusable, but it was out of his immaturity. Once he saw that he was on a new road. I wanted to join him on that road, yet at the same time knock him off it.

I learned I had to confess to Jake and ask his forgiveness. That was next to impossible. Nadine showed me it was the fear of being vulnerable. The other person can use your confession against you, but you have to ask it for yourself no matter what the other person does with it. It takes strength and will power. But it's the only way to make a new start and come to inner healing and health, I learned.

When I finally went to Jake, I was shaking so badly I could hardly talk. He knew what I was doing. He let me confess without interrupting me. I was crying. He stood up and took my hands and pulled me up from the chair. He held me and then did a typical Jake thing. He hugged me and said, 'Rhonda, I know where you are. I've been there. You feel like you're handing the other person a big stick to beat you with.'

My face was in his shoulder. He could feel I nodded. Then he pushed me back a little and said, 'Look here. I have the stick you gave me.' Then he acted like he threw it over his shoulder. 'There. Did you hear it? It landed in the river and floated away.' Then I got another of those wonderful kisses that make me float on clouds.

A huge light went on. 'Jake, you helped me realize something just now. I still have the stick you gave me here in my hand. Oh, did I ever use it. I'm so sorry! I'm so very sorry.' I bawled in his shoulder a long time. He just held me.

Then I turned to stand beside him. I imitated his toss. 'There. It's in the same river. I don't want to beat you any longer.' We both laughed and hugged. I cried a lot, but Jake never let me go or made me feel small. Looking back on it makes me see it was what Nadine called 'a moment of healing.' It certainly was that. For both of us, I think.

SESSION FIFTEEN

Thursday, 9 AM

RHONDA ASKED FOR an appointment.

R: Thanks for seeing me. (She moves around the room, then sits. Rubs her hands on her thighs. Folds and unfolds them, rubs them on her thighs again.) Can you tell I'm nervous?!

N: Would you like anything, something to drink?

R: Yes, thanks, some water … Thank you. I'm nervous and shaking but nothing bad has happened. I mean Jake is … he's just …well it's like having a new husband but the same man. He's so wonderful. Oh, he still has his quirks which exasperate me, like never folding the afghan when he uses it, or picking up his socks in the den. He can be so absent-minded about where he leaves things. He can't see the clothes he's looking for right in front of him. But you've taught me that's my agenda, not his.

But I'm chattering. The thing is … what I'm trying to say is I need to make a decision.

N: You're at a crossroads?

R: Yes. It's scary. (She looks up at me.) I feel I'm changing, too. I'm hardly ever angry at Jake the way I used to be. He's really changed, too. It's starting to be so nice coming home and to him. I don't just get a peck when I come home. I get a real kiss each and every time. He goes in to work early and comes home before I do. I like seeing him. He's so handsome I tingle when I see him. He's so tender with me now all the time and it's not like he thinks I'm fragile. I can tell he likes to be close to me at the end of the day when we sit down to watch the news and such. I can just sense his love for me, but he won't say it because of the way I used to act when he did.

He lets me sorta take the lead because I know he doesn't want to appear he's begging. Know what I mean? But when he feels I want a kiss or a hug, it's like he was just waiting for the chance.

133

Sometimes I just want to hug him and drag him off to bed with me. Still, I'm afraid it's going to hurt, it's been so long. Then I think how it used to be with him … Sometimes I want him so much it hurts. I don't know what's happening to me. I'm confused.

N: Rhonda? (She looks up at me.) It sounds like you're falling in love.

R: (Her eyes go wide, her hands go to her mouth, she sucks in air.) Oh, my goodness. You think? Sometimes, really all the time, when I see him again, I feel as giddy as a school girl. Me at my age? Fall in love? I feel like I'm just being silly and have to control it. I can lay in bed and dream about his hands being all over me. I tell myself it's just a fantasy. But at times it's so intense I can't sleep. I've got to stop the silly dreaming. Bu, I can't, somehow.

N: You try to stop it and can't?

R: (She nods her head up and down, her chin quivers.) I've shut him out for so long maybe it's too late. I don't know. (She cries openly) It had to hurt the way I abused him. Maybe I hurt him too deeply. Maybe it can only be surface things between us anymore. I have really been so cruel. I feel so guilty, so ashamed. The thing is, Jake never does anything to make me feel guilty. In some ways that's even worse. I wish he'd yell at me or walk out. I'd deserve it. (She pauses. I wait.)

N: Rhonda? (She looks up) Guilt feelings can take a long time to heal. Remember, though, what Jake did with the stick? How are you going to know how Jake feels?

R: I think you're suggesting I talk to him?

N: Do you think that will help?

R: Yes, that's what I need to do. But I did something on the spur of the moment that makes me scared when I think about it. Jake is taking vacation the whole of May. He doesn't have any real plans. Well, I booked a cruise without talking to him. I'm scared I did the wrong thing. Crazy me. I know I was testing him again when I did it. When am I going to get over that? What if he says he won't go? Then I'm really sunk. Why did I do it? If he says no? I'm afraid he'll be so angry at me he'll walk out. I would die if he did that. I want him with me more than I ever did.

N: What do you feel you need to do?

R: I need to talk with Jake, for sure. My fingers are crossed. I really need to do it, and I need to do it tonight. I just hope I don't lose my nerve. Do you have an opening for Friday? I know I'll need to come in. I am so scared.

N: Tomorrow at two?

R: Yes. Oh, right. Tomorrow is Friday. I'll see you tomorrow at two.

SESSION SIXTEEN

Friday 2 P.M.

RHONDA ALMOST bounced in

R: Why did I worry? Jake made dinner. He's some chef. After he cleaned up he came into the den. (She related the following.)

R: Jake?

J: Yes

R: I've got a confession to make.

J: Oh, oh. What did you do?

R: You know you're vacation in May? (I saw a twinkle in his eyes and he was holding back a smile) What? Do you know something?

J: Uh, you did let it lay on the dining room table.

R: And you looked at it, of course.

J: I still have eyes, you know, and there were no TOP SECRET signs around that I could see.

R: Well, will you go with me on that cruise?

J: Unless you'd rather have someone else go with you.

R: You're terrible, you know.

J: You've known that for a very long time.

R: That's not what I mean, and you know it, you bum. What do I do with a guy like you?

J: Taking me with you on a cruise would be so nice.

R: (I nearly floated out of the room, but then I turned back and plopped in his lap.) I love you, Jake Grey Millson. I really do. You've made me fall in love with you all over again.

J: May I say something? (I waited. He snuggled his face into my hair.) I love you, too. Always have. Always will. And something else.

R: Yes?

J: I know you're scared. You know what I mean, I think. Don't be. I attended some lectures at the library downtown on sexuality.

I learned some important things. You'll find out. We'll wait until we're on our honeymoon cruise, OK?

R: You're just too much, you know. Too, too much.

J: Hmm. You seem to be handling it just fine.

R: Thank you, Nadine, for never giving in to me or giving up on me.

N: You're welcome. Enjoy the cruise.

SESSION SEVENTEEN

RHONDA PHONED for an appointment. I assumed she wanted to recount the cruise. It turned out I was wrong. She was smiling and looked relaxed as she came in. How different her appearance was these days. Everything about was brighter, from her physical appearance to her choice of clothes. She was never overweight, but she was trimmer than I'd ever seen her. She was a pretty lady.

N: How was the cruise, Rhonda?

R: It was over and above. Jake is incredible. Talk about a second honeymoon ... that was it. Really, it was like a first one, in a way. I don't remember our first one much, but this one will be with me as long as I live. The lectures Jake attended must have been great. I have never felt so special in all my life. I guess we're both learning to be married adults and not married children. But that's not why I'm here.

N: I see. You've run into a difficulty?

R: Yes. In a way it's a huge one. At least to me it's huge. (She begins twisting her hands together, folds and unfolds them in lap, rubs palms on thighs, clamps jaw.) I have a fear, a huge one.

N: I see. I'm listening.

R: You'll probably laugh at me. Well, no, I know you won't or I wouldn't be here. You see, Jake has begun to attend church again. He likes it, I can tell. He's asked me to go with him but I can't.

N: Something is stopping you?

R: Yes. My fear. That's why I'm here. I'm deathly scared of churches. I did go with him one time because I thought my fear was silly. But when we got to the church steps I threw up. I was so scared I couldn't go in. Jake took me home, thank God. He didn't laugh at me. He just helped me calm down. He's puzzled, I know.

N: Were your parents religious?

R: Not really. Daddy would go sometime and take Daryll. I always begged off somehow. Mom never went. She was frail and sick a lot. When it was bad I'd get shipped off to Auntie. Daryll got to go to a friend. She was wicked to the max, this aunt. She thought I was the worst of sinners.

She was always putting me in this dark closet and locking the door. Before she did it she'd say things like, 'You got a wicked devil in you, girl. I'm going to get the devil out of you. You better pray hard the devil doesn't come get you. He'll open the big hole in the floor in there and you'll drop straight to hell.'

Then the noises would begin. I often soiled myself, I was so scared. Then it was a tub of cold water and soap that felt like fire. One time I threw up before she could shut the door. She got it all over her, too. There was a mess all over. She was some mad. She said I better never go to church. There was a big black hole under the floor right inside the door. Anyone who was a wicked sinner like me would fall through the floor into that big black hole.

One time I was crying when I had to go there. Daryll asked me why so I finally told him. He told Daddy. Daddy wanted to know why I didn't tell him. I said Auntie told me I'd die that very night and go straight to hell if I told. He went to her. I know the police were involved and Auntie Dear was put in some kind of hospital.

Daddy took me to Auntie's house and showed me what she did on the wall in the other room, on the other side of the closet. He told me Auntie was a looney. That helped some but I still can't go into a church. I know it's childish but I just can't.

N: It sounds to me that church doors are the closet door.

R: Oh, I never thought of it like that. But, now that you say it, that's what they are. When I get up close they actually look like that closet door. How do I get over that? I tell myself it's childish but it doesn't help.

N: That sounds like being parental. That doesn't help?

R: It does sound like that now you say it. I try to encourage myself. That doesn't work, either.

N: Being a coach to yourself isn't any more effective?

R: (laughs) You're right. Parenting and coaching don't work.

N: What might be a more adult response to your fear?

R: That's a good question. I'll need to think about that one.

N: We can work on that another time if you like.

R: Yes, I'll phone you.

SESSION EIGHTEEN

R: THAT WAS A difficult homework assignment you gave me last week. About the only thing I could think of was to tell myself it was a child-like reaction. I don't have to look at it that way as an adult.

N: You can set limits to your fears?

R: I tried to tell myself it wasn't going to get me, but it didn't help. Maybe I have to keep trying to make it work.

N: Yes. Fears are tenacious. Perhaps I can suggest something.

R: I'll be happy to hear it.

N: First, fears are not reality. Think back to the dark closet. Did anything happen?

R: No, it didn't, that's true. I see! You are only afraid of what might happen. My wicked aunt was playing with a little girl's mind. She knew moaning voices and strange noises will frighten a child. It's real to the child, though.

N: Besides, Rhonda, your aunt was insane. She was likely taken to a mental hospital.

R: You know, Daddy used to say she was crazy and to pay no attention to her. But you can't tell that to a little girl who gets scared out of her mind.

N: Rhonda, how do you feel about your aunt?

R: Well, I know she's mad, crazy in the head. But I am angry as I can be at her for her abusiveness. Sometimes, I wish she was dead. I wish she'd die a horrible painful death. (She sobs into her hands. I wait.)

N: Rhonda, do you think there is any connection between your anger at Jake and your anger at your aunt?

R: (Her head comes up.) You're suggesting ... I don't think ... They're two such different ... (She pauses.) I never thought about it before. But, yes, I guess I heaped on Jake everything I felt about my aunt. His abusiveness was just the excuse I needed to beat on him. I was really beating her and getting away with it besides. How terrible.

N: Jake had his faults.

R: He did. He did. But I can see now I was a ticking bomb. I was a time bomb waiting to explode. And explode, I did. Oh, how I exploded.

N: You were a little girl. You couldn't take out your anger on your aunt.

R: So it took it out on Jake.

N: Do you think you can forgive your aunt?

R: Forgive? Forgive? (A long pause.) I guess it's the only thing I can do. Forgive her. She doesn't deserve it. But, yes, I can forgive her.

N: And yourself?

R: Wow. Wow. Forgive myself? Forgive myself? I learned here I have a right to be angry about abuse, but not to do what I did about it. I know Jake has forgiven me. Really, he never held anything against me to forgive. I guess I have to forgive myself. That's the way I was, but I'm not like that any longer.

Thanks, Nadine. Thanks. It's almost like you wound me to heal me at the same time. It's like a doctor probing, hurting you to find out what your problem is. And then prescribing the right medicine to help you heal.

I know. Our time is up. I'll see you next week?

N: Next week.

SESSION NINETEEN

R: JAKE AND I talked about our last session. I told him how sorry I was for taking out all my anger on him. He did the typical Jake thing. He told me he loves me and always will. I'm stuck with him for the rest of his life. I told him I was glad. That night we made wonderful love. I have never felt so blessed.

N: May we go back to where the church doors were the closet door? You said telling yourself they weren't going to get to you didn't help. Do you recall that? Are you saying you went to a church to try?

R: Yes, I recall it very well. Jake and I went but I didn't go in.

N: Taking it step at a time?

R: Yes, that was Jake's idea. The next time push it a little farther, and so on. Jake had another idea. He wants me to close my eyes and let him lead me as if I were blind.

N: That should be tried only under specific conditions. Never with a blindfold and the leader must strictly keep his promise to stop when asked to stop.

R: It's like I should control my fear and not let my fear control me?

N: Well said, Rhonda. You should always feel that you are in control in this situation.

R: Thanks. Jake is very sensitive and kind about this. I'm sure I can trust him. He helps me without making me feel that I'm just being silly…Yes, it's time. I'll phone you.

SESSION TWENTY

N: YOU LOOK LIKE the proverbial cat.

R: I feel like that, too. Jake went with me, I think it was four times. Each time I kept my eyes closed and said the mantra. It worked. I was able to go all the way to the church door without feeling nauseous.

N: The mantra?

R: Yes. The one you taught me. 'Fear is not reality.' I felt like a child but I was determined to conquer.

N: It was now or never?

R: For sure. Then I started to think what an adult would do.

N: What was your conclusion?

R: An adult would keep their eyes open. All adults do and so do children, really.

N: Not many of them have the fear you have, however.

R: That's right. That's what I thought of, too. So I began to imagine myself without the fear. It was right then a thought came to my mind. No one has ever fallen into a black hole in a church. It would sure be in the news if it had happened. (She looks at the door.) 'Screw you, Aunt. You're gone. You're history!' (She looks back at me.) I talked over my next move with Jake first. I decided to do the steps up to the door a few times. Then, if I felt I could, I would take the handle of the door to go in. If I chickened out, Jake would leave with me immediately. I got to where I could open the door and step in.

N: How did you feel?

R: Scared to the max. I shut my eyes at first. The narthex was quite dark. Jake let me open the door to the sanctuary. When I pulled it open I saw all the colors of the stained-glass windows. The sun was at the right angle to show them all. It was beautiful. It was only when we were back outside that I realized I didn't even think about the black hole. I went with Jake to a service but couldn't get all the way through. I wasn't able to keep the queasiness down. I cried about it on the way home but Jake made me realize how strong and brave he thought I was.

N: As long as you keep doing as you are the fear will grow dimmer. Also, remembering the source of your fear will help overcome it.

R: Jake says it helped him to send his mother out the back door. Maybe I can do the same with Auntie. Forgive her but have nothing more to do with her or her insanity. She was insane.

N: Rhonda, you are doing fine.

R: Thank you. I am what I am today because of you. That goes for our marriage, too.

N: Remember? You made the phone call to come in for help.

R: True, but I did it because I was so angry at Jake.

N: You could have just left him. I believe that somewhere within your heart you were looking for help for yourself as well.

R: I guess I don't give myself enough credit, do I?

N: You have strength beyond what you realize. A weak person could not have done what you have.

R: Thank you. Daddy told me I lived through what would make most kids insane. I thought it was just a compliment. You make me see it was much more.

This is the end, I know. Jake and I will be fine. We're starting to talk our problems out. We never go to bed angry anymore, thanks to you. We're sleeping together again, as you know. It's so nice being close to him all night. I cuddle up in his arms. It's heavenly.

We talked about you the other day. We both feel that if you can use anything of our work with you, feel free to use it. We would like to be of help to others if we can.

N: I sincerely appreciate that. You have both been models in the way you were willing to admit problems and grow past them. You have my sincere good wishes. And my door is always open.

CONFESSION OF A HOTHEADED TEENAGER

I REMEMBER the incident well, all too well—like it happened yesterday. I'm into my forties now, but it still causes me some pain and embarrassment. At the same time I'm also grateful that it happened as it did.

I was a hothead to say the least. I had reasons for my anger. It seemed to me anger was all I saw around my home and often became the victim of it from parents and older siblings. As a kid I acted out a lot. I often lashed back with anger only to learn that put me on the receiving end of an even harder payback.

That's what made me angry. Why couldn't they help me with doing things right instead of getting angry all the time and criticizing? Why did I have to get hit so much? Doesn't every kid need help to learn? He can't learn on his own. Maybe they didn't even want me to be around. It sure seemed like that to me.

I could go on and on in this line, but that is a sidetrack. But still I harbored a lot of anger and resentment and I knew it. I blamed everyone else for it. Nothing could penetrate the fog I was in to have me see anger was my reaction to the situation; a normal reaction given the circumstances. But that anger was my choice? Never!

Well, one evening a bunch of us guys decided to go to the local driving range just for fun. We had a lot of fun driving those golf balls. But I had to be the best. I was, except for one other guy. He could out-hit me all too often.

I was getting mad inside but didn't let myself know it at the time. I diverted it. There was a tractor pulling a rig that picked up the balls we hit. It had a cage on it to protect the driver, so I struck on the idea of trying to hit the cage. We both got a couple of hits, but I wanted to be the only one.

Then one of the guys by accident sliced a ball that went way across the road that ran along the driving range. He was scared stiff that his ball was going to hit a car, but it didn't. Well, that gave me an idea. I started belting balls across the road, over the cars. It was fun.

About then a kid who worked for the range came up and told me the manager wanted to see me. I was the self-appointed leader of the group, so I didn't suspect anything. So I went in.

Without looking up, he said, "I forgot to tell you that there is a five dollar deposit for all the balls hit across the road. You get your fiver back when you bring all the balls back." He tapped the desk with the eraser of his pencil.

Talk about furious, that was me. I plunked the five down and stormed out the door. I knew my fiver was gone. It took me a long time to save up that fiver. I was never going to find all those balls. I went back to my spot. A few of the balls went straight. But all too many found their way across the road.

I felt a tap on my shoulder. I looked back. There stood a police officer.

"Come with me, young man!"

He took a firm grip on my upper arm and guided me out to his cruiser. He had no right to humiliate me that way in front of all my buddies. He shoved me roughly into the back seat, got in the front and began filling out some forms. I was seething. He stopped and turned toward me.

"I want your attention for a few minutes," he said, looking through the mesh between us. "You're probably as mad as you can be right now. You think you have your reasons. All of you always do. But you need to think about something. Nobody's going to pay for what you do except you. You don't have a record and you're about to get one. If that's the way you want it to be, okay. You'll go from little things to bigger ones and finally end up in jail. Is that what you want? You want to do that to your friends and family? You want to do that to yourself? You won't be able to get a decent job; you won't have any kind of life; you'll be more miserable than you ever thought you could be.

"If you land in jail, things could happen to you that you will never get over. The older guys in the pen are just waiting for a young virgin like you to come in to give them some fun.

"I'll tell you what. You think it over. If you'll go back in there and apologize to the manager, I'll bet he'll even give you your deposit back. It has to be a real apology. Like, 'I'm sorry for wasting those golf balls,' or 'I was wrong to do what I did.' You get the picture.

"If you do that and keep out of trouble for six months or so, I'll make this all go away. It's your decision. You think about it."

He returned to his writing.

Talk about a punch in the gut. That was it. He made me think things that had never entered my head. I certainly didn't want what he just described. But the thought of apologizing to that so-and-so manager was humiliating, to say the very least. I had a big decision to make.

He was getting out of the cruiser. "I'm going to talk to the manager a minute."

I made my decision. "Officer! Officer!" He looked back at me.

"May I talk to you a minute before you go in?" He nodded and sat back down.

"You're right. I was wrong and I know it. I don't want to ruin everything. I will go in and apologize." About now I was ready to bawl, but I held it back.

"OK, bud. Let's go in."

He came around to let me out. We went in to the manager. I apologized for being such a jerk and promised not to do such things in the future. And I'd spend some time looking for those balls I hit across the road.

The manager went to the till and came back with my fiver. I didn't want it and told him so.

"I'm sure not going to keep it," he said.

I handed it toward the officer. "Can you give it to the police work with kids?"

"I can't take cash." He looked at the tin on the counter.

It said something about a crippled children's fund. I put it in there.

The officer held out his hand. I took it.

"Good going, kid. I'll keep my end if you keep yours." I promised I would, but I was still mad as a hatter.

I shook the manager's hand and thanked him for what he did. I guess I meant it, at least I wanted to. About then the guys were done driving and trooped in. Back out front they all wanted to know what happened.

"I got a lecture for being such a jerk," was all I said.

They tried to play it down, but I said, "They were right and I was wrong."

No, I didn't get over all my anger immediately. It took time. Believe me, it took time. I learned real quick that I had to stay out of bars. Drinking almost got me in trouble one time.

I was in the bar a few blocks from home. I had a beer and was on the next one when this guy starts spouting off about his kid's teacher and what a jerk she was for getting his kid suspended.

I knew him and his kid. His kid was the biggest bully a school ever had and deserved getting the suspension. That kid's name was often heard at our dinner table.

What made me mad was the teacher was my mother. She had put up with that kid's crap for half a year before she turned him over to the principal. I walked up to him and was about to slug him when that cop's words rang in my ears. It was one of the hardest things I've ever done, but I finally just turned around and walked away.

I heard him ask what that punk kid wanted. Someone said, "He's no punk, you SOB. You're just lucky he didn't put you flat on your ass the floor like he could have."

I didn't hear the rest and didn't want to. I was just glad I had walked away, but I was boiling inside. My mom was about the only one in my family who was good to me. I didn't want to make her feel ashamed of me. I went for a long walk before I went back to my digs.

There was a popular young adult group in a church near where I lived. I started going there to see if there was a girl that I might like to meet. About the second time I attended the leader led a discussion on anger. It surprised me to learn that I was not the only one who had a problem with it.

He said anger is our response to a number of things. It can be from abuse, injustice, feeling neglected, or abandoned. If it starts in our childhood we usually feel powerless or defeated and we tend to carry those feelings into adulthood. We keep repeating our childhood response to it, too, as adults.

I didn't hear much after that because he was describing me! I came out of my reverie to realize that almost all the others had left. Pastor Jack, the leader, came up turned a chair backward and sat on it in front of me.

"I've noticed that you've been attending our group. Glad to have you on board. I'm Jack." He offered his hand.

I took it. "I'm Sanford, uh…Sandy Pells."

We talked a while. He seemed to sense my need but he didn't probe, thankfully.

All he did was suggest a couple of books about managing my anger. One thing that struck me in my reading most of all was this. It is not events that make me angry. Really? Anger is a person's reaction to events. My anger may be justified, my acting out isn't. I may have good reasons for being angry, but I will usually take it out on the wrong people or the right people in the wrong way. I need to learn appropriate ways to deal with my anger.

Those ideas stuck with me. I'm trying my best. Sometimes I fail, but overall I'm getting better, I think. No, I know I am.

By the way, I met my wife in that group. I love her and her even temperament. We have three boys. They are the best teachers I've ever had. I've told them that.

Jason, the oldest one said, "Sure, Dad!" One day I'll tell them why.

A TRAGEDY OF ERRORS

IT WAS A beautiful, mild fall evening—just the right weather to do some neighborhood calling. I had been taking a survey of the area to learn some of the attitudes of this community toward churches. One of the questions was, "Why do you think the people of this community don't go to church?"

As I approached the second home, its neatly kept lawn impressed me. The flowerbeds were an array of plants and colors. To the left of the curved walk that led to the front door was a rock garden that caught my eye. It was a mound of earth and rocks about three feet high. A variety of flowers had been planted on the mound. These ranged from alyssum around the border to cannas up in the center. Little ceramic figurines of elves and animals could be seen half hidden among the flowery array. The whole scene set my imagination going. These little figures began playing tag with each other. I was sorry I couldn't stand and take in the sight for a longer time.

I went to the front door. When I pushed the button I heard the doorbell chime. A man who appeared to be in his early fifties opened the door. He answered my questions pleasantly until I came to the one mentioned above. He paused. He looked past me. His shoulders sagged. While I wondered if he would answer, I was sincerely hoping he would. I stood with my pencil poised, ready to take some notes. He then looked down at my pad and pencil. I took it as a signal to put them aside, so I did.

"Y'all got an hour or two to set'n list'n a spell?" The question carried the air of a command. His Kentucky accent was strong and clear.

(Perhaps it would be helpful to translate some of his words before you read further. *Ah* = I, *'athin* = within, *hep* = help, *ornrier* = a term for naughty, *they* sometimes = there, *thar* = there, *thet* = that. Most of the other ways his accent will be evident).

I nodded. "If you want to talk, I have time to listen."

He held open the door. I walked past him into the living room.

"Y'all just set y'sef down over thar in thet big chair 'n Ah'll set here in this'n."

We sat down.

"Y'all wanted to know why Ah don't go to the church meetins?" That wasn't exactly my question, but it was the intent of it. "Ah don't rightly know where to begin. Ah live alone right now. Din't always, though. Used to have a wife and three young-uns.

"Ah were raised a right religious man and always went to the church meetins. Went because Ah wanted to go and because Ah liked it. We had different preacher-men in my time. Some was good; some wan't so good. But that din't matter none. Church was church and Ah took my place in it. Was a deacon for a couple of year afore all the trouble set in. But Ah'm gittin' too fer ahead of m'sef.

"When Ah growed up and got too big to stay on m'Pappy's place, Ah got me a farm of m'own. It was a good'un and I did right good for a couple of year. Then Ah figgered the place needed a woman and Ah needed a wife. They was a right hansome woman at the church thet Ah seed lookin' at me now and agin, so Ah went callin' at her door. Well, we was married 'athin a year and was happy, we was. She was a good woman, she was, and Ah tried to do right by her.

"We did near ever'thin t'gether, we did. Ah was used to cookin' for me an'm' Pappy asides from doin' the farm work. So Ah mostly did the brepfst an' always hepped with the dishes. Din't mind none. Now Ah din't have to do 'em alone. Besides, the hep Ah had was right nice. We did the rest of the things in the house t'gether, too. She hepped me with the farmin' and we did right good. Was payin' the place off fast like. We was three year thet way and then the first young'un came along. Purtiest little girl Ah ever did see. Mah, thet made us the proudest family in them parts. 'Member the day she was baptized, Ah do. It were a right good day.

"Then, as Ah look on it, Ah think Ah did wrong. Ah don't rightly know, but Ah think so, 'cause thet's when it all started, Ah think. A man comes along an' offers me a big price fer the farm. It took me by surprise at furst. Ah was alone when he come, so Ah tole him Ah had to talk it over with Emmy Sue. She was mah wife, then. At furst we wan't in the mind of sellin'. We had us a week to think on it, so we wan't in no hurry.

"Well, a few days later Emmy Sue sez t'me. 'Junior Redd'-- (Thet's m'name). 'Junior Redd,' she sez, 'Ah'm athinkin' you ought t'sell the place. And Ah'll tell you why, too. You know how you like mechanics. You're always doin' work fer ever'body else. And most of the time it's fer free. You have a touch fer weldin' an' such. Sooner or later y'all's goin' to have to make up yer mind. It's takin' so much time yer neglectin' the farm work. With the price y'll be getting' fer the place, y'all could buy thet gerage what's up fer sale and do yer mechanics the whole day long. It's got a right nice house with it too."

"I knowed she was right. The more Ah thought on it, the more it just fit right. So Ah sold the farm and bought the gerage and the house with it. All them new farm machines needed a lot of work from time to time. Ah din't overcharge, so Ah got a lot of work to do and did right good. Soon the men wouldn't go to no one else. They come from miles around t'get their fixin' done. Soon laid on three more men t'hep keep up with all the work comin' in. Then we had to build a bigger gerage and had to hire a bookkeeper, n'all.

"'Sides, when Ah got me them helpers, Ah had me more time fer the family, 'n church, too. Little Button, thet's the oldest, she was just startin' school an' Buddy was three, 'Emmy Sue was in a family way agin. She was needin' hep. So I went back to the gerage some ev'nins to make up the time Ah spent heppin' her. When Jacob was borned, we call him JoJo, Ah figgered we has us the best family anybody could want. They wan't nutthin wrong nowheres.

"Ah was a deacon at the church 'n hepped the preacher-man on Sundys with the meetin's. Thet preacher-man was a right good'un. He could preach up a sermon thet'd make a body set up an' listen. The church growed to where we had to build us a new one to make place for all the folks that was acomin' to the meetin's. It got so thet the preacher-man needed hep, like Ah needed a bookkeeper.

"He up and askt Emmy Sue iffen she'd take it on. She learnt typin' in high school an' can figger right good, too. So we talked it up and decided she could do that a few mornin's a week. Thet's all thet was needed and it went right good, too. We din't need the money, so we give it back to the mission we was doin' up the holler apiece. The gerage took care of us right good. We din't have no needs."

He stopped and looked at me out of the corner of his eye. "Y'all sure y'got the time fer this?"

"Yes, if you want to tell me . . . "

"Say, y're a preacher-man, ain't ya!"

It wasn't a question at all. I nodded agreement, yet feared that I would be shown the door.

"Well, preacher-man, y'all just set right thar 'n listen up, 'cause Ah ain't done yet."

Again I nodded.

He continued. "Well, thet went on till JoJo started school. Emmy Sue was working; near ever' mornin' at the church an' the preacher-man's wife was heppin part time, too. Well, then thet preacher-man took sick 'n died athin a short while. He wan't thet old nither. His young'uns was mostly growed, but he din't look nor act old. We lost a right good man. But Ah 'spect the Lord's ways is best.

"Well, ain't nobody was so griefed over it as was mah Emmy Sue, next t'his wife, Ah mean. Emmy Sue took to her bed fer days. She wouldn't eat, nor nuthin. Ah was right skeered fer her. She was a thinin' out bad. Ah was skeered to whistle, afeered she'd blow away. So Ah took me to Doc Border 'n he askt me to bring Emmy Sue on in, which Ah did. He give her a shot 'n some pills 'n told me that'd make her appetite come back. But she'd have to come in for a shot ever Monday for four times. It worked good, too. She started to come right out of it. She wan't normal fer a long time, though.

"Ah begun to think thet mebbe what she needed was to talk about Preacher-man Woods. She han't ever done thet. Ah started on it, slow like. She took to it like a duck to water. We done us a lot of talkin' on it. Found out she was feelin' about him like Ah feels about mah men at work. She was a good woman, she was.

"Right about then we got us another Preacher-man. He wan't that young but he din't 'peer t'have no 'speerience t'mount to much. He din't have much t'say in his sermons. 'N he wan't stedy like a preacher-man should be. Ah din't like the way he looked at the wominfolks. Most men din't. He din't stand t'talk to menfolks after church meetin' Sundys. Always was atalkin' to the wominfolks. 'Peered t'me he was skeered of menfolks.

"Folks started talkin'. Now they ain't no truble with talkin' to wominfolks. Ah does it too, when it's called fer. But he was avoidin' the men. He 'peered to want to get away when menfolks did talk to him. All our meetin's was hard. We never got much done. He was always needin' his own way. Acted as if we din't have no brains, he did, just 'cause we weren't edicated like he was.

"He did come avisitin' Emmy Sue a few times. He did her right good, too. She perked up an' was atakin' her place like normal in no time a'tall. Ah thanked him fer thet 'n told him so. 'Bout then he askt her to work fer him same as she did fer Preacher-man Woods. Ah din't see no trouble in it, so we decides she would. Fact is, Ah was pleased about it. Emmy Sue was needin' sumthin' t'do 'n as Ah seed it, we owed the preacher-man fer what he did fer her.

"But it weren't long afore Ah knowed sumthin' was wrong. Emmy Sue weren't hersef. Ah decides to'give her some time. Maybe goin' back to work was hard fer her. She was still pinin' fer Preacher-man Woods. Ah knowed thet. Ah could figger that workin' fer the new preacher-man weren't easy, nither. But over time nuthin' changed fer the better, nuthin' a'tall. The younguns started a'noticin' it, too. They was ornrier 'n Ah ever seed 'em be. They begun to sass back 'n not do they chores 'n all. More'n once

Ah had to lay a hand on 'em, which Ah don't like doin'. They just din't seem no other way to it. Ah was a'wantin' t'do the same fer Emmy Sue, but thet wouldn't be right.

"The real truble started when she started takin' to the bed in the spare room at the house. Ah tried to talk t'her, but they was no changin' her mind. She begun t'be right secret on ever'thin'. Ah couldn't tetch her or even look at her no more. Things was real bad. Ah was a'needin't'do sumthin', but Ah din't know what. Ah couldn't go to thet preacher-man. Ah begun to 'spect he was the biggest part of the truble. Ah din't know who to talk too. Ah din't want to go a'stirin' up no hornet's nests. Ah wan't goin' t'church no more, an' a lot of other folks wan't nither. But Ah was a'prayin' harder'n Ah bin prayin' all my life. Ah rekkin Ah got an answer, but not like Ah 'spected.

"One mornin' little JoJo comes outta school to the gerage lookin' sicker'n Ah ever seed him. Ah wrapped him up 'n took him home 'n put him t'bed 'n give him some warm milk. He went t'sleep real quick, so Ah went fer his mother. When Ah comes to the church they wan't nobody in the office. That 'peered strange t'me. Ah knowed they went to the kitchen t'have a cup of coffee, of a mornin', but they wan't nobody there nither.

"Thet had me wonderin' a whole lot. Ah decides t'look around a little. Then Ah heared gigglin' 'n laffin' 'n carryin' on in a side room. Ah tried the door but it was locked. Ah'm sure they heared, 'cause it went quiet like, real quick. Ah went back to m'truck 'n drove out, but decides t'turn around 'n go back. Well, thar they was, in the office a'workin' away as if they was havin' a fit.

"Ah told Emmy Sue Ah needed her t'come on home. She din't want to at fust, but Ah told her JoJo come home sick. Thet preacher-man acted real big-like. Told her he could get on fer the day 'thout her. Ah thought, 'You'll get on 'thout her longer'n yer thinkin' on.'

"Well, Ah was noticin' sumpthin' about Emmy Sue but couldn't settle on it right off. She was off to her car, but Ah told her to ride with me. We'd get her car later. Ah had things to talk on a bit. So she got in m'truck with me.

"Now, Ah'm tellin' this to you jest as it was, so's you get it right. It came to me what Ah was seein'. So Ah sez to Emmy Sue, 'You in a habit of late in not wearin' your underclothes?' She was about to explode, so it seemed. She got redder'n a hot stove. She askt fer me to stop, but Ah din't. Ah told her coffee time in the nursery must be fun, too. Then she really let loose. She named me fer a man whut was no man, 'cause Ah was a sneak and a blabber mouth an' cause Ah had a dirty mind'n such. But Ah just askt her why some underwear was stickin' out of her hand bag sittin' on the floor of the truck. She hit me then'n pulled on the steerin' wheel. Ah did things Ah ain't proud of. Ah rekken she'll have a scar by her mouth fer a long time.

"Well, when it all come out, she 'mitted to they goin's on. Ah askt her to quit thet work 'n stop seein' thet no-count preacher-man. She wouldn't promise nuthin'. So Ah went to the preacher-man's missus. She knowed sumpthin' was goin' on 'cause he wan't takin' to his bed at night, nither. Han't fer a long time since. Ah went to the Deacons, too. 'N thet's the biggest grief of all. They wouldn't b'lieve me nor his wife. They rekkened it were us. Thought we two was carryin' on 'n tryin' t'put it off on good people. The preacher-man took to thet real quick like. But it all came out after a'whiles. But it was too late then. The damage were done.

"The church went down to near nuthin. It were less than the one we started with. Don't know if it'll ever 'mount t'much agin.

"Ah tried to get justice, but it din't work. So Ah took things t'm'own hands.

"Thet preacher-man 'n Emmy Sue took me off t'court 'n took everthin' Ah owned, even the younguns. Ah rekken Ah was wrong fer layin' into 'em the way Ah did. Judge sed it were the law's duty to'do whut had t'be done. Ah told him Ah went to the poleece, but they wouldn't do nuthin'. He sed Ah shoulda got me a lawyer. Ah told him Ah did but he sed Ah had no case 'cause Ah had no proof. So Ah went to the preacher-man m'sef. I rekken mah boots did some real damage to his privits. So the Judge gave them all Ah owned. So Ah moved on up here t'get me a job. Ain't doin' too bad now, but Ah'll never see inside another church, Ah won't.

"Ah ain't sorry fer what Ah did t'thet preacher-man. Ah hurt him wheres he din't want to be hurt. Ain't goin' t'enjoy hissef ever agin, Ah rekken. Had t'have an operation so's he wouldn't die.

"Mah Bonnie Mae, thet's little Button, is a'comin' up soon's she finishes her high schoolin'. She's a'wantin' t'get away from her Ma. Went t'the judge on her own, she did. He give her the right to come on up 'n live with me. The boys's in grammy school, but they's a'comin' up too, soon's they can, Bonnie Mae sez. She tells me they ain't no home life left a'tall back thar. Thet preacher-man is a'drinkin' hissef t'death. Him 'n Emmy Sue don't live respectable a'tall. Least Ah kin do is hep my younguns.

"Well, thet's my story, preacher-man. It ain't purty 'n Ah ain't claimin' it's right what Ah done, but thet's why Ah don't go to church none no more. Ah still do my prayin' 'n readin' but Ah ain't fer church no more. Y'all will excuse me, but you'll have t'look fer yer sheep somewhay's else."

We sat in silence for what seemed a long time. I could not move from the chair. Finally he looked up at me. His shoulders hunched over. "Ah did wrong 'n she did wrong, but Ah would have her back any time. She were a right good woman." A tear rolled down his cheek as he shook his head.

I stood and walked over to him. He stood. I reached out my hand. He took it. I put my left hand on his shoulder and said, "God bless you, my brother. I regret that anyone who worked in the name of the Lord hurt you so deeply."

His tears ran freely while he nodded his head. "Y'all come on back, ya hear?" he half whispered.

"Soon," I said, "very soon."

THE FLY

Prologue

MR. BILLS ASKED ME, his personal secretary, to sit in on the meeting to take some notes. He said specifically he did not want them to be called minutes. I entered the meeting room with him and Mayor Megaoris. I seated myself in the chair at the far end of the table.

Mr. Mayor, (his preferred designation) while he introduced the various members of the committee, their respective places in the community and their qualifications, continued glancing toward the doors. He made a point of heartily welcoming Miss Fusbode as a valuable member of the committee. After the photographer entered to take some pictures Mr. Mayor followed him out of the room.

Mr. Bills sat in his characteristic way with his elbows on the table his hands clasped out in front of him. A pen with the point upward protruded from between his fingers. He introduced the reason for the committee and its intended goal. He suggested the meeting be conducted like a general forum, or a round table discussion. He would serve only to keep the discussion on target. He asked if anyone cared to open the discussion.

Captain Piper said, "I would like to make some remarks. First of all, the name. Homeless. The ongoing work our organization does among these people indicates the term 'homeless' is objectionable to them."

Ira Notalento interrupted, "Well, they are homeless aren't they?"

Captain continued, "Please allow me to continue. The term is inaccurate and pejorative."

Notalento said, "I don't see why it is."

Mr. Bills said, "Please allow each speaker to finish their

remarks uninterrupted. Make notes on the pads in front of you for your responses. Each person will be given all the time they need to do so. Captain?"

"Thank you, Mr. Bills. From our perspective they may seem homeless. From their perspective they are not. Their home is the street. 'Street people,' for want of a better term, is a more accurate designation. Also, we should bear in mind one hundred percent of these people are victims. Victims of physical and mental predisposition to drug and alcohol abuse, mental health issues, physical abuse, societal attitudes and their own bad choices.

"Still, the same as with each one of us, not one of them would willingly give up their home. I hasten to add they need to feed their bad habits. Having little income they turn to theft for funds to support those bad habits. That renders them criminals, those who turn to theft. In spite of all of this, they are human beings. As human beings they deserve respect and understanding. Any help we decide to give them needs to take all this in perspective. Thank you."

His remarks provoked back and forth discussion. Various views were expressed. Then Ms. Sterne cleared her throat. A general silence followed. "Captain. Your remarks afforded me a rather new perspective on the whole issue. I for one appreciate what you said. It makes a lot of sense. The wisdom of your words is not taken lightly."

Nods and voices of agreement circled the members.

It was at this point I personally became aware of the problem the fly was causing.

A day later the following article came in the mail to Mr. Mayor's office. I presented it to His Honor for review. He returned it to me without remarks. He didn't destroy it, so I am including it in the file. It does accurately describe the mayhem caused by the fly.

Phoebe Alden Rouche

THE PROBLEM of the homeless was growing in Bridgeton. Their number seemed to have increased rapidly the last few years as the economy had taken a turn for the better. These vagrants came from near and far in the hopes of sharing the trickle-down effect of the wealth. Unfortunately, as some saw it, these 'unwanteds' gravitated toward the southeast sector of the city. The vacant industrial buildings and warehouses drew the scurvy crowds as a summer beach draws sun-bathers (maybe I should say as a carcass draws flies.)

The mayor had used quite a different figure of speech. He was reported to have said "as the city offal site attracts vermin," though those weren't the precise words he is reported to have used. They were, in fact, quite vulgar. In public, though, he denied vigorously ever having such a cavalier attitude or said such detestable words. The grapevine was sure and certain it was true, bolstered by the report of an unnamed source who reportedly heard the remark. That did not, of course, make it true, but the grapevine has no concern for such niceties of discernment.

The grapevine, factual or not, did have one positive effect. It spurred Hizzoner Mayor Cornwell Megaoris, the usually lackadaisical, dillydallying mayor, into action. His usual resort to a spurious speech was surprisingly overridden by wisdom for a change. The overt spurs to Hizzoner's action are being accurately reported in what is being related to you, but to spare the feelings of the innocent, or even possibly not innocents, some language has been altered and names have been changed.

Many people were convinced that the problem arose from the new bridge the city fathers had built across the river. It flowed along the east side of city, curved toward the west before turning south again. The grant they sought from the state had been approved, so the old bridge that was a mile farther south had been replaced by the new bridge in the sector of the city just mentioned.

The merchants hailed it. The flow of traffic that carried goods and services to and from the city was greatly enhanced. Popular opinion, however, was definite that the bridge should never have been built in the first place. The city fathers should have foreseen that the many nooks and crannies created by said bridge would inevitably be another attraction for 'people like that.'

Terrestrial soss they were called, or ethnic argol, again not the terms used, but the meaning was the same. And, though the presence of these so-called human whelps was an actual infringement on the rights of very few, if any, the local citizenry and businessmen began to clamor for a solution to 'the problem.' Something needed to be done and quickly. The mayor stoutly affirmed that the upcoming election had no influence on his decision 'in any manner whatsoever.' The fact that he voiced this was taken as proof of the exact opposite.

Since this is a factual report and not a political harangue, this writer needs only to report that Hizzoner Mayor Cornwell Megaoris appointed a committee to 'study the problem and report back to him posthaste' which a local paper loyal to the mayor dutifully relayed to its reading populace.

It was two o'clock on a hot July afternoon. The duly appointed seven were beginning to arrive. The meeting took place in the largest bank in the center of the city. Manfred (Manny) Bills, the president of said bank, had been appointed to the committee and had graciously offered the use of the bank's large air-conditioned second-floor conference room. The shiny mahogany table in the center of the maroon carpeted room could easily seat twenty persons in the padded armchairs that lined the walls—until meeting times. The table was rectangular in shape with convex sides, or it could be called ovate, with flat ends. These ends left room for only two of these padded armchairs.

Because of Mr. Bills' generosity Mayor Megaoris had also appointed him to chair the meeting. Seven chairs had been drawn from the walls and set around the near end of the table. The double doors to the room were set in the left wall, about one-fourth of the way along from the corner. Thus the chairman could see with ease anyone coming through those doors. The chairs were arranged three on each side and one at the end. An agenda for the meeting had been placed on the table in front of each chair. A tablet and a retractable ball-point pen each boldly embossed with the bank's logo had been added. A name card with the member's name lay on top of each agenda.

Ms. Vera Sterne, a local university professor, dressed in her conservative brown skirt suit, and Laurence (Lorry) Shipper, president of a local trucking company, clad in gray company uniform with its logo on the right pocket and a Dickies© label stitched above the left pocket, happened to arrive simultaneously and rode the elevator to the second floor in silence. Ms. Sterne's graying hair was pulled back in a bun that rode on her suit collar. Their seats were the second and third ones to the left of the chairman.

Captain Yma C. Piper, in his Salvation Army uniform, entered the bank next, took the stairs to the second floor, entered the room, found his designated place, which was the third seat to the right of the chairman, placed his cap on the table and seated himself. Immediately after Floris B. Kinder, chair of the local JC's entered and seated himself at his designated place immediately to the left of the chairman. Floris had on light blue shirt that topped dark blue trousers.

Then Commissioner Ira Notalento entered and took his place next to Captain Piper. He toted a kind of handleless satchel that was supposed to make him look like a busy and important man, but his rumpled non-descript clothes betrayed him. At the stroke of 2 PM Manny and Cornwell entered together, both dressed in black business suits and monochrome ties. Manny took his seat at the head of the table. Corney (i.e. Mayor Cornwell Megaoris) chose to stand next to Manny since he did not intend to be an ex officio member of the committee.

Corney looked at the closed door to his left and the empty seat immediately to Manny's right. He shook his head, cleared his throat and was about to speak when the knob on the left of the double doors rattled. Sixteen eyes turned automatically to said rattle. It rattled again and then opened as if by itself. Then the figure of a woman appeared in the doorway and, as if she had been ushered in, swept into the room. It was none other than

Clairelea Fusbode (pronounced, she insisted, Clair-RAY Foos-bow-THAY). Clairelea could not have chosen a more precise moment to gain the full attention of the entire assemblage. From her appearance and dress the conclusion was inescapable this was the entrant's desired, if unadmitted, intent.

Clairelea was not tall. If she topped five foot three it would be by a sixteenth of an inch. Her bouffant coif was supposed to make her look taller but it only attracted negative attention. Now, it would be unkind to say that Clairelea was obese, but were she to lose twenty pounds the size ten clothes she wore would fit her figure and person more precisely. Her maroon skirt was stretched so tight across her derriere it looked as if the threads in the seams were ready to give up the fight to keep the seam intact. Besides, the pink blouse's low-cut bodice was just short of obscene. It revealed artificially created mounds and its resulting deep cleavage. The buttons on that blouse had to strain so hard to perform their common task, it was difficult not to feel sorry for them. (Of course, any physical assistance to them was out of the question.)

Clairelea wore shoes with four-inch heels that put her back in such a curve it would be the envy of a long bow. Besides, those shoes made her walk with a little hop that any rabbit would find difficult to duplicate. The final touch to the gaudiness was the faux fur stole that was draped through her elbows and behind her back.

Clairelea paused momentarily, raised a delicately gloved hand to her lips as if in sincere apology for the disruption her tardiness caused. The empty chair to the immediate right of Manny was obviously the only chair she could assume.

Instead of passing directly behind Hizzoner and Manny to said chair Clairelea flounced and bounced her way down to the far end of the table and then rustled her way to the vacant space and paused until Ira Notalento perceived the hint, stood, pulled the chair back for Clairelea to seat herself. He pushed the chair toward her just quick enough to cause her to plop unceremoniously onto the seat. The men seemed to be shuffling papers, writing hurried notes, clearing throats, or settling in more comfortably as this entire process labored to its conclusion. Vera's eyes were fixed on the table in front of her as Clairelea ostentated to her chair, but her cheeks were unusually pink.

While this procession was winding to its conclusion Manny dutifully proceeded to close the door.

Corney began the meeting by introducing the members of the committee and giving a long-winded spiel about his deep concern for the homeless and his 'desire to see something done about their plight.' (It must be said that the citizenry of Hizzoner's city seemed to have a much larger 'plight' than the homeless.) He and the Town Council 'were expecting an early recommendation from the committee.' A local press photographer slipped in at this point, took a couple of shots and disappeared. Within fifteen seconds Hizzoner had turned the meeting over to Manny and also disappeared.

Manny led the meeting well. The discussion was going nicely. The mood was generally amiable. It looked as if prospects for an early report were more than favorable. But those hopes soon dwindled appreciably and finally were rendered impossible, as we shall see.

No one in the room could have told you, if you had inquired when Fly first made its presence known. But that it was there was beyond question. It was not one of those flies that would willy-nilly flit here and there creating a general nuisance, though that would have been bad enough. This was one of those big lazy flies that took its time. It was probably the peskiest fly that ever existed. As Fly lit or flew away, its wings beat furiously for a mini-second inciting an involuntary reaction to the resulting annoying tickle, a slap at the hapless intruder, depending on where it had decided to land. Yet, for all its apparent lethargy, Fly was peculiarly adept at evading the intended crushing blow. The slapper only succeeded in slapping him or herself where Fly had left the annoying tickle.

Fly buzzed around a few heads first to make its presence known before it made its first landing. That was on Captain

Piper's nose. The Captain's reaction was to simultaneously swish Fly away with his hand, blow at his nose with his lower lip extended and shake his head furiously. His glasses were nearly dislodged by his reaction. He managed to prevent their fall and red-faced pushed them back into place. Even Vera Sterne could hardly suppress a grin as low chuckles circled the table.

After bedeviling Captain's nose for a few more minutes, Fly took leave for better pesting grounds. That was nothing other than Chairman Manny's balding pate. The siege lasted all of five minutes. The first attack was Manny's initiation to the presence of the nettlesome bullyragger. Now he knew firsthand what was happening to his committee and capturing everyone's attention. But, try as he would, he could not divest himself or his committee of the misery Fly was causing.

Fly swooped low over Manny's head a few times as a plane would reconnoiter a bombing site. Fly barely grazed the fuzz that still grew on Manny's balding pate. Then it harassed Manny's ears and face while Manny's fanned with his hand, hoping to convince the persistent invader that its continued interest in his person would of surety lead to its doom. Fly was not so easy to convince.

The first actual landing of the invader took place in the fuzzy area on the back of Manny's head. It was just above the denser part of his remaining hair which lay draped like an ermine stole over his ears. Manny's head lurched forward at the forcibleness of the attack. It was so involuntary yet so noticeable that Lory had to pretend that he dropped something on the floor so he could work off an attack of the giggles under the cover of the table. With the amount of coughing that suddenly erupted a visitor would have concluded this group was suffering from a sudden attack of a rare strain of influenza.

At the same time that his head lurched forward, Manny's hand flew to the back of his balding pate which gave him such a slap that his head fell even further forward. He regained his outward composure quickly enough but the redness of his face betrayed his true feeling at one and the same time about himself and the invader. The break in the flow of his thoughts was fully evinced in his halting attempt to regain the essence of his speech. Try as he might, it simply eluded him.

Unfortunately, Fly was not done with Manny. It proceeded to land again on the same ermine strip, this time just above Manny's left ear. It then crawled slowly from there down into said ear and tried to burrow itself into the fold at the top edge of this auditory enhancer. All the while Fly's wings were beating furiously, as was the habit of this ill-behaved miscreant. It successfully evaded Manny's slap, as is needless to say. But the way Manny cocked his head, slapped his ear in an effort to dislodge the untoward usurper, left some in the meeting unable to retain their composure. To their credit only Vera and Clairelea did not show outward mirth.

Manny's efforts did dislodge Devilkin, but unnoticed it landed on Manny's collar and began to crawl around to the front of Manny's neck. It seemed to spy some delicacy there and jumped at it with wings aflutter. It not only took the morsel but a tiny bit of Manny's skin in the process. The miniature archfiend's luck nearly ran out with that unkindly act. Manny's hand was so swift and so accurate that had it not been for the space between Manny's fingers The Siege would have come to an end then and there. But, its luck having held, Fly apparently decided not to press his good fortune and try it elsewhere.

Elsewhere was to parade down the middle of the table in reckless abandon. It was too inviting to ignore. Lory, Ira, and Floris each took a swipe at Fly with rolled up agendas, but (need it be added?) missed.

It was uncanny how such a small vagrant could hold so many full-grown and right-thinking adults completely captive. The situation was fast becoming more than intolerable. But short of adjourning the meeting and calling in an exterminator, no one knew exactly what to do.

Floris later said that he seriously thought of going out to beg, borrow, or steal a pistol to take care of Intruder. On second thought he had dismissed the idea; it might have made the situation more disruptive than already was.

Then it happened. No one could have thought of, surmised, or foreseen, or otherwise predicted what was about to ensue. Once it did happen, its logic was as clear as the light coming from the dozen fluorescent tubes beaming from the ceiling. Fly headed for what must have been the original object of its pestment.

Surely, all previous objects of its affectations were just that, mere affectations. The object Fly sought out was nothing less than the mounds and valley Clairelea had created by her bussed-up bosom. But the manner in which it eventually landed there obliterated all doubt that this was Predator's original intention. Though it did not arrive at this destination in the manner it must have originally planned.

Its initial approach to its happy hunting ground was not a bold and brazen advance. It began by buzzing her ear. Clairelea was thoroughly nonplussed by this antic of Fly. If anyone had been able to read her mind (though most of the time it was incomprehensible even to Clairelea), that person would have discerned that Clairelea was convinced that she of all people was immune the attacks of the miniature monster.

In her view, such a foul creature could not be possessed of the audacity necessary to inflict itself and its demonic behavior on her person. But this determined devilkin was not a respecter of persons in the slightest degree. Had it been able to read Clairelea's mind, its determination would only have been increased. It was sparing its best for the last.

After first failing to outwit Fly by ignoring it, Clairelea was at the point of taking action when Fly moved its playground from her ear to the area of her coif just behind her ear. Miscreant's mistake became immediately clear. It became entangled in the sticky substance in Clairelea's hair that kept the coif intact.

Fly was stuck. All the while Flippant's wings fluttered ferociously in an effort to free itself from the sticky prison. Clairelea gave Flippant's desire an unexpected boost when she stealthily moved her hand to her coif as if to tame a stray tress. She extended her delicately gloved fingers momentarily to accomplish her mission.

The action freed Fly from its pokey, but not from Clairelea's finger. The goo on Fly's feet became affixed momentarily to Clairelea's glove. At the wrong moment its fluttering freed Fly, but being unable to fly landed unceremoniously onto the exposed area of Clairelea's bulging bosom. As it landed, wings still aflutter, it fixed its sticky feet on that exposed skin and took a vengeful bite.

With an unmuffled "Oohe", Clairelea half rose from her chair as she swished at the molester with a prettily laced hankie. The unwelcome lodger was dislodged but the luck of the vulgar vagrant had all but run its course. It fell ignominiously into the bosomic crevasse Clairelea had created. With wings still aflutter it descended into the darkness of this heretofore untraversed territory.

Clairelea met the buzz created in her bosom by Fly's fluttering and nipping with uncommon unappreciation. Her "Oohs" were interspersed with "Deah mees" as she swished vainly with that hankie in desperate hopes of convincing the vulgar vagrant to betake itself from her person now and forever.

To his credit, when Chairman Manny saw that she was at the point of descending into that crevasse with her fingers to oust the uninvited and unwanted guest from its lodgings, he promptly adjourned the meeting. He was afterward heard to remark that he sincerely wished he had followed an earlier impulse to halt the meeting until Fly could be given his due reward for its untimely invasion.

All the members passed out hastily except Vera. She paused at Clairelea's chair to lend assistance, for it looked as if Clairelea was about to pass momentarily from consciousness. Even if she did not faint clearly Clairelea was in no position to manage on her own.

Clairelea's final action before she swooned was to thump her midsection a time or two with her open palm. A miniature cloud of talcum floated out. As suddenly as it had begun the buzzing in her bosom ceased, to Clairelea's late but utter relief. Vera assisted her to the Ladies Room.

What transpired there we are not told, nor did anyone inquire. The two reappeared sometime later, though Clairelea was still as white as a newly bleached bed sheet. They entered the elevator and after exiting the front door merged into the crowd of shoppers.

Manny reported to Corney that he was sure a new committee should be chosen in view of the day's events. Corney agreed to do so but never did. Rather, he sent the police to keep the poor unfortunates from trespassing on private property and from being a public nuisance (neither of which had as yet occurred). Eventually many of them left the city. Hizzoner was credited with having 'done a fine job.' Though the city was rid of the bulk of the problem, not a few realized that nothing constructive had been done. Cities elsewhere would be forced to deal with Bridgeton's 'flies'.

Late that fateful day the cleaning lady took over the meeting room to do her chores. She sighed deeply and sat in one of the chairs extending her feet in front of her. After a few moments she pushed herself up and said on rising, "Thank God it's the last one for the day. Ten hours six days a week to make enough to live on is too much."

She then busied herself with the cleaning of the room. Just as she was about to dust the table, she noticed a small whitish object lying near what was the chairman's end. Closer inspection revealed it to be a nearly dead fly. It was barely able to crawl and looked to be burdened down with a powdery white coat.

As she looked at the hapless fly she said, "'Pears you been where you hain't ought to be. Where that was I don't know. But you shore fixed yoreself up good this time. I only hope you enjoyed it while it lasted."

She was thinking that the white powdery stuff was perhaps from some sugared donut or sweet roll. Little did she realize the truth of the matter. With that she crushed the fly with her dusting cloth and swept it onto the floor. A few moments later the dust bag of her vacuum cleaner became the final resting place of Fly's earthly remains.

End Note

Perhaps a word or two about Clairelea's person and situation would be in order.

Clairelea was the only child of Mr. & Mrs. Stearner Percival Kaptol. There was some persistent gossip about her paternal progenitor. Clairelea bore none of her father's looks or personal characteristics. Stearner Percival was reported to be a less than ideal husband and father, though he was an excellent businessman. His dry-goods business thrived under his leadership. His employees had high respect for him and he treated them very well. He rewarded their industry with higher than average wages and generous bonuses at each year's end.

Her mother died when Clairelea was nine years old. An aunt saw to her upbringing as best she could. Her father died just as she turned eighteen. The circumstances of his death were the talk of the town. His body was discovered by a maid in a local hotel room early one morning. He was fifty-two. The door of the room stood ajar to her surprise and she noticed some woman's lingerie on the floor near the open door. The doctor/coroner certified that Stearner died of a heart attack. No further investigation was made. Upon his death Clairelea legally changed her name to her mother's maiden name.

Stearner willed enough of his estate to Clairelea to provide for her for the rest of her life. That was probably his only creditable act of fathering he ever did. It could well have been from guilty conscience, though that would have been rare indeed.

He knew Clairelea lacked ability to be a good student. Many heard him make remarks on that subject. She was pushed from grade to grade all the way from elementary through high school. She enrolled in Junior College and after three years the institution decided to give her a certificate of attendance.

Clairelea accepted her 'diploma' with great pride. The managers of the few jobs she did land soon found various reasons to reorganize their staff and find Clairelea's 'capable services' were no longer required.

After that she wished, whined, and wheedled her way onto various committees around town. She was on the board of the local museum, the library, the Art Institute, and the Park Beautification Commission, to name only four. Her dress at these meetings was no less spectacular (should I say gaudy) than it was as mentioned above.

Much more could be written, but in the interest of fairness, the writer deems this to be enough to give the reader some understanding of, if not sympathy for, Clairelea's person and character.

P.A.R.

THE CATAPULT

A true story

IT HAPPENED toward the end of the Second World War. Our family lived on a farm in central Iowa, in Jasper County to be exact. My oldest brother was in the military, serving in the Pacific Theater. The other two brothers older than I were working at other jobs. That left me to help with some of the farm work. That had its limits because I was fourteen at the time and was small for my age.

Our farm was two hundred and ten acres. A quarter section is a half mile square and comprises one hundred sixty acres. Our farm had an extra thirty acres that lay along the left side at the back. If you looked at the farm from the air, it would have the shape of a backward upside-down L.

An artesian well at the northwest corner of the farm provided water for the stock tank. An underground pipe from the well brought water to the stock tank near the barn. The pipe wound along the base of the rolling hills to reach the barn area. It was nearly a half mile long. It had been laid that way years before to allow the water to flow by gravity from the spring to the tank since electricity was not available and a gas engine was not feasible.

The pipe split in places and over time roots clogged it. It stopped working. There was a small well near the house, but it was not deep enough to supply all the water needed for the stock. Pa bought a three-hundred gallon tank that he put in the buckboard wagon. A buckboard wagon is one that has huge wheels in the back that are nearly five feet tall. The front ones are a little smaller. The result is the box is around three feet off the ground. It was like the one in the picture but without the spring seat.

The tank took up most of the space in the wagon box. There was just enough room in the front of the tank to allow a person to squat sideways. That's where I was going to sit. Pa had asked me to go with him to help pump the tank full. He backed the tractor up to the wagon and positioned the end of the tongue onto the draw bar, then slid the pin through the aligned holes. I opened the big wide gate in the fence. After Pa pulled through I shut it again and took my seat in the wagon.

High gear in those early tractors was slow, it was four or five miles an hour. To save time Pa shifted to neutral at the top of the hill just beyond the gate to coast down. The tractor hit a bump at the top and the pin jumped out of the holes. The wagon, set free as it was, headed down the hill on its own. The path curved to the left but the wagon didn't follow the path. It went straight down the hill. It started to gain speed. I watched from my narrow perch as the tongue of the wagon bounced along the ground.

I have never been so scared in my life. I was sure the tongue or a front wheel would hit a rock, a small mound or a rock which would cause the wagon to yaw sharply. That was sure to make the wagon turn over. I didn't know what would become of me if that happened. In my fear I stood up and began to yell to Pa for help. He motioned for me to sit down, but I was having none of it.

I thought of crawling across the tank and dropping off the back, but was afraid I'd be shaken off because the wagon was bumping and swaying over rough ground. Those big churning wheels looked like killers ready to crush me to death. Even if I made it across to the back, there was an eighteen inch long spigot sticking out the back. I was afraid I'd get caught on that. So I stayed standing scared stiff and yelling for Pa to help.

Near the bottom of the hill the long tongue went into a slight depression. It stuck into the ground which made the wagon come to a jolting halt. The wagon didn't want to halt. The result was the front of the wagon bucked violently into the air. That shot me out like a rock from a catapult. I remember screaming as I flew into the air, but then I must have blacked out.

I was flung about fifty feet and landed on the grassy flood plain along the creek bed. The next thing I remember is crawling up the bank with my hands on both sides of my head screaming, "My head's broke. My head's broke." I was sure it was split in two. I was certain the only thing keeping it together was my hands.

Pa was sitting on the tractor seat with his head leaning on his arms on the steering wheel. He said later he was wondering how to tell Mom he had just killed a son.

He jumped down when he heard me screaming. He said something and tried to take my hands down but I wouldn't let him. I was sure my head was going to fall into two pieces if I let go. He made me lay on the grass and rest. He spoke to me again, but I didn't hear it or couldn't understand it. My head was hurting too much. I think I fell asleep.

The next thing I knew Pa was talking to me and asking me how I felt. I woke up. By that time I was feeling a little better. At least I knew my head was not broken. But it felt like I had been in a deep sleep and couldn't quite wake up.

When Pa had me lay there on the grass he went to the machine shed for a chain. I saw he had pulled the wagon free and had it hooked up to the tractor again. I was going to sit in the wagon again, but I saw I couldn't. When the wagon stopped so abruptly the tank slid so far forward in the wagon box that there wasn't even three inches left between the tank and the front of the buckboard. Had I sat down as Pa wanted me to I would have been crushed to death.

I sat on the rear axle housing of the tractor, which was wide and flat, the rest of the way to the spring. Pa wouldn't allow me to do any of the pumping. He asked me a few times if I had a headache. I assured him that I didn't. He seemed surprised. The only thing I remember is feeling that my head wouldn't quite clear up. I don't remember the trip back to the barnyard.

When Pa told Mom about the incident she made me stay in the house. She didn't want me to do much of anything the rest of the day. It happened to be a Saturday. She had me stay home from church the next day and had an older sister to stay with me to be sure that I stayed quiet.

When I woke Monday and went down to the kitchen, Mom asked how I felt. I assured her I felt quite normal again. None the worse for wear.

POEMS

I Had a Love

I had a love—she lovely was—
  A lightsome joy to me.
I lost the love that lovely was;
  She was too young for me.

I had a love—she kindly was—
  A love that set me free.
I hold the love that kindly was
  Deep down inside of me.

I had a love—she pretty was—
  I mourn her loss to me.
I see the love that pretty was
  Drift far away from me.

I had a love—she friendly was—
  So open, warm, so free.
I know that love that friendship was
  Will ne'er be a loss to me.

So come, my love – that truly was—
  Come, walk and talk with me.
We'll freely walk and joyly talk
  With ne'er demands from me.
We'll part. I'll hold my heart.
  We'll part away, both free.

The Lane

(His Wedding Vow)

I trod a tree-lined lane today
Where sun-crusted snow lay
In patches. Rivulets frozen deep
In ancient ruts up the steep
Hillside warned my feet beware,
"Feet poorly shod will not fare well here."

When springtime thaw exiles snow and frost
I'll trod the lane at greater cost.
The clinging soil
Make heavy feet and greater toil.
But spring will yield to summer climes.
I'll trod this lane in freer times.

When lovers trod a lane together,
Life is easier in any weather.
Feet fall more safely when
They're brac'd by a friend.

So come and walk through life with me.
We'll trod this lane together.
Our love will brace and comfort be
When comes the stormy weather.
'Twill also help us joy the sun
Or sandy beach in summer fun.
Our feet will fall more safely when
We keep love alive until the end.

I Loved a Maid

I loved a maid,
but young was she.
I loved this maid
and she loved me.

We walked, we talked;
we were quite free.
I loved this maid,
but young was she.

To a 'Valentine'

Your soft brown eyes look deep
Into the soul of me, I fear,
Noting every fault and weakness there.
Yet your friendship's given free.

I bare my inner soul to you,
Crying out in agony and pain.
Answ'ring hug: a soft refreshing rain.
Gentle caress: the rose's morning dew.

Your soft brown eyes have come
To bless me recently, I know,
Soothing away the pain of long ago.
My feet easily find their home.

I'd not paint you perfect—'tis unfair.
The gift you have you've given me:
Your kindness from a heart so free.
Such love's a treasure rare.

This poem reflects the result of counseling with a young man. He felt empowered by the decision he made to take control of his life. After the last session he walked out with a light step and a smile that lit his face.

She Won My Heart

She won my heart
E'n from the start.
She sat across from me

She knew my heart
E'en from the start
Would ne'er quite beat free

She seemed content
And e'en quite bent
To let me captive be.

And all the while
She'd smirk and smile
Knowing well she toy'd with me.

Till one day
She deigned to say
"I am in love with thee."

But on that day
Forced was I to say
Your toying set me free.

Reflecting made me think
I teetered on the brink
Of love-sick's insanity.

Your toying bold
Freed your hold.
I will respected be.

A Friend

A friend is a beautiful blossom
On a warm spring day.
Beautiful. Fragrant. Free.

Its blushing aura entices. Stay,
Life beckons.   must away...
Pledges. Duties. Tasks.

I tuck away its fragrance...
Pocket it deep in memory.
Sweet. Soothing. Serene.

Returning, the tree's in full fruit.
Its taste gives full delight.
Calms. Pleases. Satisfies.

The blossom's been transposed
Yet remains the same.
Beautiful. Fragrant. Free.

Marilynn Smith, a fellow resident, asked me one day at breakfast, "What are the signs of spring?" I asked for a page from her pad and wrote the following:

Signs of Spring

Returning birds,
Greening grass,
Disappearing snow are
Signs of winter's pass.
Farmers plowing fields
While dreaming of
Harvest yields.
Noisy big machines,
Cows beginning to calve,
Leaves and blooming trees
Hearing children play and laugh.
These are signs of Spring.

My First-born Son

I hold my first-born close to me
Sensing new responsibility.
How can I be equipped, I ask
To carry out this fearsome task
Until he walks free.

I gave his life to him
Thinking not in lover's whim,
I cast a future life to lead.
Give me strength I plead.

I hear his crying in the night.
Seek him out in dimmed light.
Satisfy his raging thirst
Watching sun's new burst
Upon my first-born son.

POEMS (BLACK)

PREFACE

The poems on the following pages were written after I experienced a bleak period of my life. This happened in the late 1990s and the first two years of 2000.

I trust the poems are self-explanatory. My reason for including them is to tell readers who have experienced deep pain and despair to not give up hope, seek counsel, and plod onward toward new light.

Dark And Deep

Dark and deep the forest where
  The mind is lost in bleak despair.
E'en hope is not a word
  By which the god-cursed soul is stirred.

This mortal life gives joy nor pain
  And no desire for light again.
The soul is one with crumbling clod.
  "Accept this flesh into your sod."

The thirsty sod now drinks the blood
  That flows into its solitude.
Leave this flesh to rest alone.
  All substance in this life is gone.

Joy rises now with coming peace.
  Rest, O soul, in its embrace.
This waning breath is ebbing fast.
  Peace and calm will call at last.

Lost At Sea

My ship lost mooring while I slept
  And drifted out to sea.
There are no maps or charts or gear
  Upon this ship with me.
    I'm lost at sea.

Nor am I a sailor trained.
  E'en did I have the gear
I'd not know how to read or plan
  To find the land from here.
    I'm lost at sea.

The wind may blow me o'er the swells;
  The stars shine clear and bright.
I know not how to read e'en these
  To guide me through this night.
    I'm lost at sea.

My ship is sinking 'neath the wave,
  Soon will I be quite free.
These swells may be my body's grave
  They'll not be grave to me.
    I'll not be lost at sea.

The Pit

The deep black pit
    Is yawning at my feet again.
Its dizzying eddy
    Unfoots and I'm sucked in.
Its horrors engulf
    My soul. 'Condemnation'
From unbodied voices
    Deepen my diminution,
Assuring me of
    Everlasting damnation.
I cannot bring
    Myself to care of 'saved' or 'lost'.
This life I'm in
    Demands too high a cost.
Would you give up
    Your mind, joy, peace, your all
Just to fulfil
    Your divine call
to stay alive?
    I cannot bide this hellish hole!
Condemn me not,
    Lord, I am coming home to whole.

Quandary

I say my prayers. I read the psalms.
Still filled am I with fears and qualms.
Where this elusive peace and calm?

Walk In My Shoes

Dark and deep the forest where
A mind is lost in black despair.
E'en hope is not a word
By which the god-cursed soul is stirred.

The cure of this vile cursedness
Is the bless'd sleep of death.
I loathe life while death you hate.
Suicide to you is devil's fate.

It is my release complete
From groveling at Satan's feet.
My escape's no more a sin
        Than 'scape from any woes I'm in.

Bide your woes! You bid me bide mine.
Platitudes and sermons are unkind.
Dare you walk with me in this despair?
'Twill take you where you do not dare

To walk. You'll run from me as if
From death itself. You'll make a rift
"Tween you and me. You'll fear the worst:
Being curs'd by my curse.

Dare you hear my anguish and my pain?
Need I intone it once again?
I beg you leave your judge's stand.
I need a friend who'll take my hand.

The Dawn

The walls before and on my sides
Halt me on my path.
A tunnel left oblique appeals
No more than marsh aback.
I'm robbed of life in forc'd choice.

Insatiable pit dark with pain—
I scream against its black abode—
I sought for help I did not want.
His voice the raging storm or'erode.

Hope's reborn in his strong voice.
This cloud-enshrouded day is lived
In borrowed strength
And hope from him who is
My counselor and friend.
His warm and tender strength
hold me to life.

I wake. Easter sun is full aglow
Upon a flowered field.
Marsh and tomb have vanished!
Awake! I did not yield
Nor perish in the strife!

"Rest a day to find the gear and will
To top the rocks and cliffs
You yet will find within your soul."
Thru him I gather self-belief.
Lusting pit can sheath
Its whetted knife!
I cling to life!

Despair Revisited

I look back upon those days
And recognize the deepening haze
That drifted on my soul and mind.

I sailed out upon that sea
And cast about if I could see
The wreck'ed ship that once was me
But found only fading memory
    Of deep despair.

I wandered thru that forest bed
Where once I longed to shed
This useless mortal coil.
The breeze that rustled thru the trees
O'er head drew my gaze to see
The Deep Blue Hope.
And I am free.

To a Friend

I lived in walls—castle thick.
I spoke only through the porthole of my profession.
You called to me. I would not hear.
Wounds were deep.
I could chance no more.

You said, 'Invite me in
to dine with you.'
Those 'mighty' walls shook and I with fear.
Ignoring walls and fear,
with ease you stepped inside.
I tried to hide.
Though you stayed warm and near.

I kept you in the back roads of my mind.
Dare I unlock my cloister's door to you?
When you sat table across from me,
Your eyes
Were warm and free.

The ice encasement of my soul
Began to melt. I feared the flood would
Sweep me off to where I dared not be.
You sat carefree on my couch
and I imprisoned -
In my
chair.

Unknowing, you dared me leave my fear
Behind and walk out to rediscover
Hope and joy.
Your kindness calmed and healed
My ragged heart.

My new-built castle claims doors not few,
I come and go at will in peace with you
Because you are a friend,
dear
and
warm
and
true.

ABOUT THE AUTHOR

Alan Arkema is a country boy, born on a farm near Lynnville, Iowa, seventh of what would eventually be twelve children. In such a family, playmates were built-in.

Arkema decided at age five that he would not become a farmer. At the end of his sophomore year in high school, he decided to become a minister. His parents were pleased.

He graduated from a denominational college and seminary (now Calvin University) in Grand Rapids, Michigan, in 1954. He married Lorraine Hofstra in August of 1951 and became the father of seven children.

Arkema spent forty years in full time ministry and another twelve part time. He served in South Dakota, Iowa, Australia, Long Island, New York, New Jersey, Ohio, Montana, and Grand Rapids, Michigan.

Since retirement, he spends time writing, painting, and woodworking. More recently, his hobbies include building 3D projects and puzzles. The most notable one is the 3D model of the Taj Mahal.

In 2019 Arkema published his first novel, *The Letter, the Memoirs of Thomas M. Woodham*. He published *Silent Sam and Other Stories* at age 95.

Other Titles by Pearl City Press

Married, Living in Italy by Misty Urban

The Last Voyage of the Marigold by Dan Moore

The Adventures of Bobby, Iowa Farm Boy by Bob Bancks

Penny and the Woodland Fairies by Bob Bancks

Escape on the Silk Road by Dan Moore

Books by Writers on the Avenue

Winter Holidays in the City of Pearls

Climbing the Hill of Life

From River to River

Everything Old is New Again: 30 Years of WOTA

Roads We've Taken